721 SECRETS

Keeping you up to date on all that goes on at Manhattan's most elite address!

A Marriage Proposition?

They say hate is one step away from love. It must be true in the case of 721 Park Avenue's twelfth-floor residents Trent Tanford and Carrie Gray. Around the building, Carrie has been known to gripe about her next-door neighbor's late-night bimbos who mistakenly knock on her door while looking for the millionaire playboy. Now rumor has it Trent may be ready to propose. We can't wait to see mousy Carrie tame the wild beast! Coincidentally, the senior Mr. Tanford is just about to retire from AMS, his media holdings. Could it be Trent thinks marriage will win him the CEO slot? And what does Ms. Gray get in the alleged deal? Just the sexiest, hottest lover this building has ever known. If this "merger" goes through, Maintenance will be called up to the twelfth floor to turn down the heat. But at 721, you're never sure what's rumor, what's scandal and what's the white-hot truth!

Dear Reader,

You must be hungry for more New York! I know I am.

This series has been such a pleasure to work on. With "killer" story lines and five wonderful authors, I was in writer heaven.

My story in particular turned out to be one of my favorite books of all time. It's funny—when I first looked at the characters of Trent and Carrie, I saw them as merely the playboy jerk and the girl next door, but as time went on, and as I started writing them, creating their dialogue, they developed in ways I hadn't imagined they would. They actually started fighting me, fighting how I wanted to write them. They pushed me to write their way, where their characters should go and who they really were.

This was a new experience for me, and just a little bit intimidating. But after a while, I learned to let go and allow them to be who they wanted to be...good or bad, wrong or right. And I'm thrilled with the results.

I love hearing from you all, so don't be shy. Let me know what you think of Trent and Carrie. Of course, if you don't approve of them, I'm afraid they have only themselves to blame:-)

All the best, friends!

Laura

LAURA WRIGHT

FRONT PAGE ENGAGEMENT

Published by Silhouette Books
America's Publisher of Contemporary Romance

What a wonderful opportunity to work with five amazing women. Barbara, Maureen, Jennifer, Emilie and Anna— you are the apples of my eye! (pun intended)

Special thanks and acknowledgment to Laura Wright for her contribution to the PARK AVENUE SCANDALS miniseries.

SILHOUETTE BOOKS

ISBN-13: 978-0-373-76885-1
ISBN-10:   0-373-76885-0

FRONT PAGE ENGAGEMENT

Visit Silhouette Books at www.eHarlequin.com

Printed in U.S.A.

Recent books by Laura Wright

Silhouette Desire

Locked Up with a Lawman #1553
Redwolf's Woman #1582
A Bed of Sand #1607
The Sultan's Bed #1661
Her Royal Bed #1674
Savor the Seduction #1687
Millionaire's Calculated Baby Bid #1828
Playboy's Ruthless Payback #1834
Rich Man's Vengeful Seduction #1839
Front Page Engagement #1885

*No Ring Required

LAURA WRIGHT

has spent most of her life immersed in the world of acting, singing and competitive ballroom dancing. But when she started writing romance, she knew she'd found her true calling! Born and raised in Minneapolis, Laura has also lived in New York City, Milwaukee and Columbus, Ohio. Currently she is happy to have set down her bags and made Los Angeles her home. And a blissful home it is—one that she shares with her theatrical production manager husband, Daniel, and three spoiled dogs. During those few hours of downtime from her beloved writing, Laura enjoys going to art galleries and movies, cooking for her hubby, walking in the woods, lazing around lakes, puttering in the kitchen and frolicking with her animals. Laura would love to hear from you. You can write to her at P.O. Box 5811, Sherman Oaks, CA 91413 or e-mail her at laurawright@laurawright.com.

Who's Who at 721 Park Avenue

6A: Marie Endicott—Her recent death is still under investigation. Police are starting to question other tenants, particularly Trent Tanford.

9B: Amanda Crawford—The cheerful event planner has a few secrets of her own.

9B: Julia Prentice—The society girl has gotten married to the infamous Wall Street millionaire Max Rolland…and there's a baby on the way.

12A: Vivian Vannick-Smythe—The building's longest-standing resident, who has been on edge lately. Could it be planning the celebration of the building's landmark status, or something else?

12B: Prince Sebastian of Caspia—This royal is about to return to the States. Housesitter Carrie Gray is hard at work maintaining his home.

12C: Trent Tanford—The playboy's next venture is neighbor Carrie Gray.

Penthouse A: Reed and Elizabeth Wellington—Planning an anniversary party for a marriage that may not last another year.

Penthouse B: Gage Lattimer—Billionaire…who may not be as reclusive as one thinks.

One

…wire one million dollars into an untraceable offshore bank account…or else your past indiscretions will be exposed…

In the center of his steel-and-suede office, Trent Tanford leaned forward in his chair and tossed the letter into the trash. He felt no anger, no concern, just a desire to get back to work. He was no stranger to threats— e-mailed, snail-mailed or otherwise. He'd received them from his father; from recently fired and subsequently pissed-off employees of his family's media empire, AMS; from women, past lovers who had refused to accept the end of a relationship.

The threats were irritating, yes. But impactful?
No.

The thirty-one-year-old media mogul knew who he was and what he wanted—in business and in life—and no amount of outside influence was going to change that.

Trent signed a stack of contracts as outside the floor-to-ceiling windows to his left, the sun crept up the horizon bringing with it a hot new August day and an office building buzzing with activity.

"Good morning, Mr. Tanford."

Trent's door was open, as it usually was before 7:00 a.m. He nodded at one of his new young executives as she passed by, a pretty and brilliant redhead who had just graduated New York University the previous year. He glanced at the clock on his monitor. "Six-thirty. Good for you."

"Yes, sir." She smiled an ultraprofessional smile and moved on.

Trent went back to work. She was pretty, but he never dipped his pen into the company ink pot, not to mention the fact that she was way too young. But he did like redheads. In fact, he had a date with one tonight. A woman who was just as pretty, but not nearly as brilliant. Which was fine. Trent sniffed as he recalled their date the previous evening. The woman had spent twenty minutes assuring him that Mitt Romney was no politician, but was in fact a famous baseball player.

Trent grinned. He loved women. He loved the way they laughed, smelled, moved—each so different, yet so similar in their belief that she was going to be the one to change him, the one to bag him, the one to make him so deliriously happy he'd forget all about that ultrastrict dating code he'd followed for the past ten years: four weeks maximum then all ties cut.

Why didn't they get it? Why couldn't they understand that he'd never come to heel? He'd never be bagged. In his past experience, Trent had learned the hard way that in four weeks a woman could become more than a casual distraction, and going there again was unacceptable at this point in his life.

Trent moved on to his computer and the must-see lineup for the following year. He was no insensitive ass when it came to his view of relationships. He was always up-front about the four weeks, and what *not* to expect from him. It wasn't a personal attack on anyone; it had nothing to do with a woman's beauty or her personality. It was simply a fact, a rule of order…and, maybe, if Trent was forced to admit it, a way for him to have his cake and his ice cream and his steak and his candy and eat it, too—without getting a raging headache afterward. A relationship headache that would keep him from his one and only desire—his ascent to president of AMS when his father retired.

Now, much to Trent's chagrin, his father subscribed to a very different view on the matter of relationships. According to James Tanford, a wife and children stabilized a man, made him stronger. A family made a man more open to power and in turn made him respected by his peers and competitors. In the man's 1950s view of things, a wife took care of the details and let the husband focus on the real issues.

Unfortunately, the senior Tanford believed this so completely that after several failed attempts to coax his son into settling down, the older man had resorted to memos referencing the subject. This last one Trent held in his hand. The memo had been placed—by one of his father's faithful minions, no doubt—under one of Trent's computer monitors, a warning that James might decide not to step down as head of AMS until Trent was settled into matrimonial bliss.

Or matrimonial hell, Trent mused darkly.

Yes, threats came to Trent's office in all shapes, sizes and media.

All in a day's work.

Trent tossed the note from his father into the trash, watching as it settled beside another crumpled ball of BS on the bottom of the trash bin—the one that demanded he wire a million dollars into an untraceable, offshore bank account on Grand Cayman Island if he didn't want certain unsavory actions from his past revealed.

Something as likely to happen, he mused, as über-bachelor Trent Tanford taking a bride anytime soon.

It was Sunday brunch in the Big Apple. A sacred event for most Manhattanites, who worked sixty-hour work-weeks and used Sunday midmornings to continue to de-compress before they started it all over again on Monday.

Normally Carrie Gray celebrated brunch with pastries, eggs, bagels, schmear and, if it were appropriate, booze. Unfortunately, she'd been too tired to set up such a feast for her friends that morning. Hell, she'd barely had enough time to stick her long, brown hair up in a ponytail. And forget about contacts. It was glasses all the way today.

After a late night working on a few sketches of a logo concept for a graphic design job she was trying to land, she'd been woken up by another member of "Trent's Troops."

Trent being Trent Tanford, the dark-haired, blue-eyed, dimple-cheeked tall drink of water who lived in the apartment next door, a man who had constant guests of the female variety coming and going at all hours of the night. These were his "Troops." The name had been invented by Carrie and her two girlfriends, Amanda Crawford and Julia Prentice, who were good enough friends of Carrie's to allow her to bitch about her annoying neighbor.

The problem was that some of Trent's lady friends hadn't learned how to read yet and were mixing up Carrie's pad, 12B—the Upper East Side apartment she house-sat for European businessman and prince, Sebastian Stone—with 12C, Trent's apartment at 721 Park Avenue. And last night around 1:00 a.m., another of Trent's size-zero glamazons, complete with red hair and plump lips, had come knocking.

"Again, I'm sorry about the spread," Carrie told her

two beautiful blond friends as they sat around the glass-and-wrought-iron coffee table in Sebastian Stone's uncluttered but artfully furnished three-bedroom apartment.

Amanda's gray eyes flashed in a friendly, teasing way as she crossed her long, thin legs. "No worries. Coffee and doughnuts are classic."

Julia touched her growing belly and added, "And these glazed ones are my baby's favorite." Four months pregnant, Julia had occupied apartment 9B in Carrie's building, until she moved in with her fiancé, Max Rolland, last month. Now her previous roommate, Amanda, had 9B all to herself.

Relieved at her friends' forgiving words, Carrie watched the pair as they downed their doughnuts in ten seconds flat, then reached for another. It was so funny. Julia and Amanda couldn't have been more different from herself. Both blue bloods, both graduates of the chichi Ivy League school Vassar, both impeccable dressers.

And then there was plain old Carrie with her green eyes and mop of dark hair, her big breasts, curvy hips and a very anti-high-fashion tie-dye hippie dress. She was okay, cute maybe, but nothing like her stunning, fabulous friends. And she was fine with that. Carrie had no insecurities about her looks or background. She was who she was. And Julia and Amanda couldn't agree more. The socialite and the event planner didn't care about Carrie's lack of looks and breeding or her lack of funds. They just wanted her friendship.

"Besides a chicken sausage quiche and an arugula salad I really wanted to make cinnamon rolls," Carrie told the two women in between sips of coffee. "But the dough's rising time and mine didn't mesh well today."

"It's no big deal, Carrie, really," Amanda assured her. "Did you have a late night?" She grinned, her makeup-free face model perfect. "A date, maybe?"

"No," Carrie answered with a laugh, as if that was the silliest question in the world. And then she stopped and wondered why that would be so silly, and how long it had been since she'd had a date. Had it been in this millennium? Sure. A year, maybe, before her mom was diagnosed…

Her blue eyes narrowed, Julia broke into Carrie's thoughts. "Let me guess. Another late-night visitor?"

"She said she didn't have a date, Jules," Amanda said, reaching for another doughnut.

"I didn't mean a male visitor," Julia clarified. "I was talking about a member of the 'troops.'"

Amanda nearly choked on her doughnut. "Oh, no. One of Trent's ladies came by?"

"Yes," Carrie said, falling back into the beautiful oak Glastonbury chair.

"The blonde again?"

"Redhead."

Amanda shrugged. "At least the guy's versatile."

But Julia wasn't about to be so relaxed about the whole thing. The woman may have been petite in stature, but she had the temper of a protective tigress when she saw injustice. "Carrie, this is total insanity. You need to confront him."

"I know," Carrie said evenly. And she did know; it was just that—

"Or at least put a sign on your door," Amanda joked, pouring herself another cup of coffee, her short blond hair falling about her face.

Julia shook her head. "You swore if another woman came looking for Trent, you'd—"

"I know, I know," Carrie said quickly. She was just embarrassed at her own lack of fortitude in the situation. "I've never had a problem with confrontation before, but this guy…Trent Tanford…he's like…I don't know, too good-looking. Those cute dimples on such a fierce face…it's off-putting. He's like the boy in high school you had a massive crush on and made sure you wore your blue eye shadow and Love's Baby Soft perfume for every day in case by some miracle he noticed you."

Julia lifted a brow. "The boy you had a crush on? Trent is like the boy you had a crush on, Car?"

"I just mean that he's that good-looking, that charismatic, that crush inducing if one was to talk to him or get to know—"

"Do you want Trent to notice you?"

"No." Carrie released a weighty breath. She was doing some major backpedaling here. "I mean, only for the purpose of telling him off."

"Because if you do want to meet him, talk to him, whatever, all you have to do is knock on his door."

"Yes, Jules, I know," Carrie said drily.

Clearly ensconced in her own world, not hearing much of Carrie and Julia's exchange, Amanda sipped her coffee and looked dreamy. "I remember that boy. But it wasn't Love's Baby Soft. It was Patchouli oil."

Carrie and Julia both turned to stare at Amanda, then burst out laughing. When Carrie got hold of herself she said, "Incidentally, that boy never did notice me except to point out when I had a fresh pimple."

"Honey," Julia interjected, "no doubt that boy is now the Fry King at your local burger shack."

"Actually I heard he plays football for the Indianapolis Colts."

"Well, I'm sure he's been rejected by many a cheerleader, then."

Carrie sighed. "I doubt it. Guys like Mr. Touchdown and like Trent, they go their whole lives never hearing the word *no*." She shrugged. "I just don't get it. What makes a woman get all nuts for a man like that? A guy who's arrogant, who's basically just after sex?"

"The tall, dark, rich thing is pretty powerful," Julia said drily.

Amanda nodded. "For some women it's the dating trifecta."

Carrie rolled her eyes. "I'm being serious, you guys."

"So are we," Julia said tightly. "To some women, some people, looks and money are everything."

Sipping her lukewarm coffee, Carrie thought about what her friends had just said, and how naive she was to even argue the point. She understood the realities of the world. It's just that she had a hard time believing that most women, at their core, wouldn't want more substance from their men. Money and looks were great, but they didn't last. They didn't rub your feet when you had a hard day's work. They didn't care when you got a small, but substantial new job. They didn't sit by your side and help you remember your past when you were going through the first stages of Alzheimer's.

Carrie brushed off that last thought. She wasn't going to bring her own baggage into the conversation. Instead, she got up and went into the kitchen, made more coffee.

An hour later, the women were standing at the front door, satiated and thinking about what was next on the Sunday to-do list, what they needed for their Monday morning and the week ahead. They thanked Carrie for the brunch, made some tentative plans for a drink later in the week, and were about to walk down the hall when Julia stepped on something outside Carrie's door.

She bent and picked it up. "Here you go." She held out a copy of the *New York Post*.

Carrie shook her head, but took the paper anyway. "It's not mine. I'm a *Times* girl." She glanced at the name on the sticker above the paper's headline.

Amanda grinned widely. "Mr. Tanford, I presume."

Carrie shook her head. "Unbelievable. Not only do I have to redirect his women, but I have to deliver his paper. I'm so ready to rumble."

"Hey, I think she's fired up, Jules," Amanda said, grinning.

"Finally." Julia squeezed Carrie's arm and whispered, "Go get him, tiger."

"Grrrr," Carrie called as the two women walked down the hall toward the elevator.

Trent had just laced up a new pair of running shoes and was checking out the high octane playlist he'd downloaded on his iPod yesterday when there was a knock at his door.

"Just a sec," he called, walking into the hall, distracted by the strange and unwelcome addition of Yani to his iTunes playlist.

When he swung the door wide, he saw a petite woman in her midtwenties standing there. She was wearing a tie-dyed dress with the same color grass-green as her eyes, which incidentally were veiled behind a pair of tortoiseshell glasses. Her long, brown hair was pulled back into a ponytail and her full lips were set in a pissed-off line. She was cute, curvy and he had seen her in the building before. "Hello."

"Hi," she said, without even a hint of a smile.

"I know you," he said, cocking his head to one side as if that would help him place her. It didn't. "How do I know you?"

She rolled her eyes, shook her head, then thrust the *New York Post* at him. "Here you go."

"Mine?"

"Yep."

She didn't say much, but there was something about her. Maybe it was the way her lips moved. He could watch that for a while.

He took the paper from her. "Are you the paperboy?"

"No."

"Good because it's two o'clock in the afternoon, and if you were the paperboy I'd have to fire you for being so late."

"That's not very nice."

"No. But I'm not very nice."

"Good to know."

"You live in the building?"

This question made her smile. Not a happy smile, but a knowing, almost irritated one. "Down the hall actually."

Oh, yeah. "Right." He grinned. "So, why was my paper delivered to you?"

"Habit, most likely," she said drily, those pink, plump lips remaining parted as if she were going to say something more.

When she didn't, he repeated, "Habit?"

"Your paper isn't the only thing that gets lost by way of my door, Mr. Tanford."

Mr. Tanford. That wasn't good. No women, except the ones who worked for him, called him Mr. Tanford. He racked his brain trying to recall a reason this particular woman might have for disliking him. It took him a moment, but then it dawned on him. His female guests, late nights...wrong apartments. He leaned against the doorjamb, arms crossed over his chest. "Twelve B, right?"

She nodded. "In the flesh."

Heat stirred inside him at her words. Hell, he was male after all. "So, you and Sebastian Stone are…"

"I'm his house sitter," she clarified, her green eyes flashing.

Women with fire, women who didn't like him, women who were totally and completely unaffected by him were few and far between.

Not his type, but he'd definitely have to see her again.

"Thank you for the paper," he said. "And I apologize for the frequent late-night intrusions. I meant to come by and apologize in person."

"Sure you did."

"I've just been busy."

"We're all busy, Mr. Tanford."

"Of course. And again, I apologize. I'll make sure my guests know exactly where to go from now on. But if not, please don't hesitate to stop by again and give me another kick in the—"

"You think this is funny," she said curtly.

He dropped the easy, lighthearted air. "No."

"Yes, you do."

"I assure you that I do not think being woken up in the middle of the night is funny," he said in all seriousness.

She lifted her chin. "Good."

"Unless it's for a very, very good reason."

Her eyes narrowed and she looked ready to pop him

in the stomach. "I expect you to take care of this problem immediately, tonight."

"I don't have a date tonight."

She exhaled loudly. "Maybe you could supply your guests with a map." She paused, then said with light sarcasm, "Or maybe not. They always seem a little flustered with directions."

He liked this woman. Liked her a lot. Maybe he needed to broaden his scope of women. "Do they?"

She nodded. "I actually had to walk one of them to your door."

He grinned. "What can I say? Smart girls don't go for guys like me."

She sniffed, looked away. "Yeah, right," she muttered under her breath.

"Excuse me?" he said, even though he'd heard her. Hell, any excuse to watch those lips move.

"Nothing. I've got to go." She gave him a wave, which sort of resembled a military salute, before taking off down the hall.

"Thanks again," he called after her.

She glanced back. "I'd say anytime, but I'd be lying."

He chuckled. "Hey. Wait a second."

"What?"

"If I see you in the hall or the elevator…"

"Yes?" She arched her brows.

"Can I call you 12B?"

This time she smiled, a real smile, a playful smile. "Not if you expect me to answer."

His mouth turned up at the corners. "What is your name?"

"Carrie Gray."

"You a smart girl, Carrie Gray?"

Again, the smile. "I'm afraid so."

Trent watched her walk back to her door, her round, firm backside swaying from side to side as she moved. Part girl, part woman. Very nice. She was pretty, sexy in her way—but definitely not his usual fare. He hadn't been lying when he'd said that smart girls didn't go for him. It wasn't that he didn't love smart women or love to be challenged by them, but right now he had all the challenge he could handle at work.

For now, he wanted uncomplicated and simple.

He walked back into the apartment, dropped onto the couch and opened the paper, completely forgetting about the run he had just been amping up for before Little Miss Next Door had shown up.

He flipped through the paper. News first, then sports. *Damn Yankees and hiding injuries. Loses credibility, loses respect.*

Disgusted and pissed off at his favorite baseball team, Trent turned the page—and got an eyeful.

"Shi—" he muttered.

Large and loud photographs of himself and Marie Endicott, the woman Trent had dated a handful of times—the woman who had jumped off the roof of his apartment building over a month ago—stared out at him from the Entertainment section of the paper.

The headline read: Suicide Victim Canoodling With AMS Playboy Right Before Her Death?

Trent tossed the paper aside and grabbed his Black-Berry off the glass coffee table. As expected, his e-mail box was flooded with requests for interviews, statements and several more pictures of him and Marie.

"Dammit."

Ten minutes later, the phone rang. It was the police with a request for an altogether different kind of interview.

"Mr. Tanford, we'd like you to come down to the station to answer a few questions."

Two

From age fourteen to age seventeen, Trent Tanford had run with a questionable crowd. Perhaps it was the sheltered, yet pampered life he'd lived with two absent parents, a pressure cooker of a prep school, and one overly protective nanny, but when puberty set in, he found himself battling a magnetlike attraction to trouble.

Under the guise of retiring to his room for homework and a good night's sleep, he would stuff pillows under his blanket and sneak out of the window. He hung out with the boys from town, proving his antimoney, anti-establishment claims by drinking too much, knocking down mailboxes and hot-wiring cars.

It wasn't long before he found his way to the cold, unfriendly walls of the police station.

Needless to say, having to pick his criminal son up from jail was not a proud moment for James Tanford. Before Trent had given up on a relationship with his father, he had actually looked at those car rides home from the station as a way to spend some time with the man, even if it consisted of a stern lecture and a slap or two.

But those years were barely recognizable to Trent now. These days, he was all about the earned dollar, and when he walked into the police station that Sunday afternoon, he sported no fear and had nothing to hide. He had, however, brought his attorney.

Trent was confident, not stupid.

"Thank you for coming, Mr. Tanford."

"Of course." True, it was a pain in the ass to be in the police station on a Sunday afternoon, but he'd liked Marie Endicott. While there had been no chemistry between them, she was a decent person, and he felt bad about what had happened to her. And if he could help, he would.

In a boxy room with overbearing fluorescent lighting and scuffed, faded walls that had once been painted yellow, Trent and his attorney, Evan Wallace, sat at an unsteady card table across from the tired-looking cop in his forties.

Detective Arnold McGray's anemic green eyes flicked over Trent with curiosity and what Trent easily recognized as a premature disbelief in whatever it was that Trent might have to say.

The questions came at him, emotion-free and quick.

Detective McGray held up a copy of the *New York Post*, which Trent had been reading earlier. "Did you post these pictures yourself?"

"No."

"Did you date Marie Endicott?"

"Yes."

"How long?"

"A few times."

"Could you be more specific?"

Trent paused. "Twice."

"Why did it end?"

"It never started."

"Why? She wasn't into you?"

"We weren't into each other."

"It's not easy to be rejected. That must've pissed you off."

Wallace interjected quickly. "This is ridiculous. Mr. Tanford dated the woman twice. Move on, Detective."

Trent silenced the attorney. "It's fine, Wallace."

McGray stared at Trent. "You're used to getting any girl you want, Mr. Tanford."

"Is that a question or a statement?"

"Men like yourself don't take kindly to being rejected."

Trent tried to make it simple. "We had nothing in common. There were no hurt feelings on either side."

"How do you know that?"

"We talked about it on our second and last date, laughed about it in fact. She said she preferred a regular working man to a careeraholic."

The questions continued along the same lines after that—Trent's feelings about Marie and hers for him, where they had gone on their dates, et cetera. As expected, Wallace continued to interrupt with his concerns and the detective continued to push.

Finally, when Detective McGray wasn't getting the answers he was looking for, he moved on to a question that had Trent sitting up straight like a riveted schoolboy.

"Have you received any threats lately? E-mail? Phone calls? Letters?"

"Yes."

Wallace looked up from his BlackBerry. "What? I was never informed—"

Trent continued quickly. "I got a letter."

Detective McGray sniffed. "What did it say?"

"The sender wanted me to wire one million dollars into an account in the Caymans or they'd expose something unseemly from my past."

"And what could that be?"

Wallace gave Trent a sharp, stop-talking-now look. But Trent had nothing to hide, and nothing to do with Marie's death.

"Not a clue. That's why I threw the letter away. I thought it was a joke."

"What do you think now?"

"I think someone wants me here talking to you about Marie's death."

The detective got up, excused himself for a moment and left the room. Trent narrowed his eyes at the door. What the hell had the letter said?

While he was waiting for the detective to return, his cell phone rang.

"What a fine position you've put us in, Trent."

His father. Trent turned around and glared at Wallace, who just lifted his brows before returning his attention to his BlackBerry. Clearly Trent needed to hire his own counsel from here on out. The company attorney had an allegiance to James Tanford first and last.

Trent released a breath. "Hello, James." Trent hadn't called him Father in over fifteen years. And he hadn't used the word *dad* ever.

"I had assumed the days of phone calls to jail were over," the man muttered.

"I'm not in custody. I'm answering a few questions."

"About the woman you were seeing."

"The woman I dated a few times," Trent clarified with mild irritation.

"A woman who died last month in a very shady way. And now there are pictures of the two of you all over the media."

Trent refused to defend the fact that he had been caught up in a coincidence. "What is it you want, James?"

"I want to know how you could be so careless?"

"I dated someone, and she just happened to be suicidal. I hardly call that careless."

Facts wouldn't override the scandal of it for James

Tanford, though. "I want an end to all the speculation and gossip. Now."

Through gritted teeth, Trent muttered a terse, "As do I. Anything else?" He and Marie had only dated a few times, but her death had affected him, and his father's cold way of making her life, her death, into a pain in the ass for himself disgusted Trent.

James sighed. "I'm not going to try and reason with you anymore, Trent. Talking doesn't seem to work with you."

"You're right about that."

"You have a choice to make, and twenty-four hours to make it in."

When was the damn detective coming back? Trent wondered darkly. He didn't have time for this. "Ultimatums and threats don't interest me."

"This one might. With AMS at stake."

Trent chuckled bitterly. So his father was going here again, was he? Damn threats. What the hell? He was practically swimming in them lately.

The older man's words came slowly, like arsenic-laced honey from a bottle. "There is one thing that might salvage our family's good name and business reputation."

"What? Firing me?"

"No. A wedding."

Trent cursed. "This is hardly that big of a scandal."

"A very white wedding."

"We're not here again." As if a really stellar wife could clean up Trent's bad-boy image.

"This is my company," James continued, "my life's

blood, and I will not allow this situation to spin out of control. Advertisers will be all over this, and I won't have any of them walking because of your foolish actions. If you are as devoted to this company as you claim, then you would do anything it takes to keep AMS on top and scandal-free."

Trent said nothing.

"You can be as cavalier as you want to, my boy, but this is a onetime offer. I will secure your future position as head of my company in writing, today, but you must be married by the end of this week."

Trent said tightly, "I will be head of this company because I am damn good at what I do. No one can touch me and you know it."

"Right now I don't care how good you are. Damn you, Trent. Do you care anything for your family's name?"

"You won't like the answer I give you."

James paused, then said tightly, "Announce your engagement by midnight tomorrow night and I will announce your new position to the company executives and to the media. Ignore my desires and I'll take that as your verbal resignation."

Fury coursed through Trent's veins, making him almost unable to see through the fogging glass pane and out into the hallway where the detective was on his way back into the room. "I'm hanging up now."

"One more thing. This woman you choose cannot be your usual fare. Permanently tanned bottoms and jiggly implants are fine for play, but this is a life partner, a

Tanford. She doesn't have to come from money, Lord knows I didn't, but she must have brains and class. Choose wisely."

"Goodbye, James."

"Do you need me to contact Wallace?"

Trent's jaw was as tight as a 7:00 a.m. subway ride. "I think he's already contacted you."

Just as Trent pressed the end button, Detective McGray walked in. Both he and Wallace took their previous seats at the table. The detective lifted his brows.

"You had an expungement as a juvenile."

"Is that a question?"

Wallace jumped in quickly. "Mr. Tanford's records are sealed and not for—"

Trent stopped him, then asked the detective, "What do you want to know?"

The man stared at him without blinking. "How bad a kid were you, Mr. Tanford?"

"Not that bad. But I gave it my best effort."

Trent's easy comeback garnered a half-ass smile from the detective and a nod. Again, he stared at Trent for several seconds, as if he were trying to decide whether to continue down that road or not.

Then he dropped his gaze and leaned back in his chair.

"You're not the only one who's gotten a letter."

That fact surprise Trent. "Who?"

"Someone else in your building."

"You're not going to tell me who?"

"It's not important. What is important is that you tell me everything you can remember about the content of that letter."

It was close to five that evening when Carrie stood on the corner of Seventy-seventh and Second Avenue and hailed a cab. She couldn't really afford the fare, but it was a muggy ninety-eight degrees out and she just couldn't deal with the subway. Plus, she was running late and needed to get to her mom's house and relieve the health-care worker before she had to pay the woman overtime.

Carrie jumped into the cab and tossed out her mother's TriBeCa address. She had tried a hundred times to get her mother to move in with her, as Sebastian Stone had graciously offered, but Rachel Gray would have none of it. Her rent-controlled TriBeCa one-bedroom was the love of her life. It had been their first apartment when she and Carrie had moved from Upstate New York almost twenty years ago. Rachel would get highly agitated if she was away from her space and her things for too long. Carrie wasn't about to force the issue of moving.

The solution was to make her mother as comfortable as possible as she battled through her disease.

Carrie let herself into her mother's apartment with her key. As always the first thing she saw was her mother's artwork on the walls. It ranged from bold to simple, and covered nearly every inch of space. Art was the reason they had moved to the city. Well, one of the reasons…

For fifteen years, Rachel Gray had enjoyed a pretty amazing career. But like any artist, when she stopped producing, the influx of money stopped, as well. She still received payment for any newly sold pieces, and had been smart with her savings. But in Manhattan, that was hardly enough.

Carrie gave the health-care worker, Wanda, who was in the kitchen preparing dinner before she left, a friendly wave, then she walked into her mother's room. It was just as it had been for as long as Carrie could remember: antique lamps, barn-wood armoire that Rachel had brought with her from Albany, photographs and knick-knacks, books on a crowded bookshelf, several original abstract paintings on the walls, some her own and several of her artist friends' work, as well. In the middle of the room was a queen-size iron sleigh bed with garish red bedding and purple throw pillows.

Carrie went to sit beside her on the bed. Tucked under the bright red comforter, Rachel had her dark brown hair piled on top of her head. Her pale face looked drawn. She had always been thin, but now she looked unhealthy. After so many years of coming through the front door after school to hear the blaring sounds of Depeche Mode as her mother hovered over a canvas, brush in hand, Carrie always needed a moment to secure herself in this reality.

Rachel stared at her, her bright hazel eyes searching. "You look like my daughter."

"I am your daughter."

"What's your name?"

"Carrie."

Rachel smiled softly. "Just like the girl on *Little House on the Prairie*."

"That's right. That's who I was named for."

"How nice."

"I think so."

Clearing her throat, Rachel sat up a little. "I'm thirsty."

"I'll get you something to drink. Be right back."

Carrie left the room, immediately missing the soft scent of herbs and mint that had always seemed to emanate from her mother's milky-white skin. Hell, she missed a lot of things. The first time Rachel had said, "You look like my daughter," Carrie had escaped into the bathroom and after several quick breaths had vomited into the sink. It was something a daughter was never supposed to hear from her mother.

Fortunately, not every day was a bad day. Some days were great. Some days Rachel knew exactly who Carrie was. Those days were gold star, blue-ribbon days.

When Carrie returned, she smiled at her mom and handed her the tea. "Here you go."

Rachel looked as though Carrie were trying to hand her a lit bomb. "I don't want that."

"You love iced tea."

Her brows knitted together. "Do I?"

Carrie nodded.

"All right then." She drank the entire glass, then began chewing on the ice cubes. She glanced up and frowned at Carrie. "Who are you?"

Carrie took her mother's hand. "I'm Carrie, your daughter."

"Good." She chewed her ice, then said, "Read to me?"

Yes, some days were worse than others.

Carrie took the book from the bedside table and began to read. She read while her mother ate dinner, then as she dozed off to sleep. But when she left a few hours later, she couldn't remember one word of it.

It was close to nine when Trent stepped into the elevator, his coat slick with rain. He'd left the police station a few hours ago, but instead of heading straight home he'd caught a quick dinner.

As the elevator was about to close, someone stuck the handle of an umbrella between the metal doors, causing them to stutter, stop, then reopen.

Trent nodded at the woman who walked into the elevator. "Hey, 12B."

When the pretty brunette lifted her head, saw who was addressing her, she rolled her lips under her teeth, giving him a really half-assed smile in return. "Hey."

As the doors closed, he took in her dejected expression and wet, moplike hair, the ends beading with rainwater. "Get caught in the storm?"

"Definitely," was the sharp reply.

"You okay?"

"Fine."

Trent watched her as she tried to dry her long dark hair with a tissue from her purse. She was no flashy, in-your-face beauty, but with her pouty lips, small, curvaceous body and don't-mess-with-me attitude she had this thing, this quality about her that made Trent want to pull her into his arms, drop his head and kiss her. Kiss her until she relaxed and forgot about whatever was making her act so pissed off.

Maybe a good, solid kiss would make him forget about his afternoon, too.

He leaned back against the elevator wall, and attempted to curb some of the irritation he felt coming from her. "Sorry."

She looked over at him, confused. "For what?"

"The 12B thing, when you got in the elevator. I was just playing around."

She looked away, then looked back at him and shook her head. "It's fine. I'm just having a hard time with people forgetting my name today."

"Work thing?"

"No. Personal."

"Guy thing?"

A small smile touched her lips. "No. Just personal."

Personal, huh? He shifted against the wall. But not a guy... Why did that fact interest him at all? "Well, I didn't mean to compound the problem. I was just trying to inject some humor into a pretty humorless day."

"Bad day for you, too?"

"Yup."

Carrie felt like a limp, wet dishrag standing there in the pristine enclosure of the elevator, and the fact that she probably also looked like one at that moment made her want to get away from this beautiful man ASAP. She tried not to stare at him in an obvious way, but it wasn't an easy trick. Trent had also been caught in the rain, his hair and face wet, but he looked amazing, even better than he had earlier in the day when she'd dropped off his paper. How was that possible? How was it possible that she looked like something the cat threw up and he looked like the cover of *Men's Health?*

She fought the urge to ask him about his crappy afternoon, swap sad stories. After all, she hardly knew the guy, and she really didn't want anyone else's burdens on her right now. Odds were that Trent's issues were about as deep as some hot blonde who stood him up because she'd managed to score an interview with Karl Lagerfeld.

When the stainless-steel doors finally opened, Carrie gave Trent a small wave, then walked out of the elevator and toward her apartment. She knew he was behind her, close behind her; she could feel him.

"How about a drink? A glass of wine?"

She didn't turn around. She did, however, shiver. "No, thanks."

"You look like you could use something."

She could. But she feared that the thing she needed wasn't alcohol. She was in her lonely phase—a phase she went through a few times a year when her life wasn't going as planned. Tonight she was going to get the pound cake out of the freezer and as she ate through its unthawed buttery goodness she would try to forget how she didn't have a job yet, how her mother was never going to get better and how she, Carrie, might have to get used to being alone permanently. Then later she would move on to the salty snacks and the memory of how good the weight of a man had felt on her once upon a time, how his hands had moved over her skin with a light touch, how his lips had felt on her temple, her ear, her navel.

She was finally at her door. Thank God.

Again she gave Trent a wave. "'Night."

"Wait a sec."

Stupidly, she turned around. The doorknob pressed into the small of her back. "What?"

"I don't know." He stood there, all a hundred and eighty pounds of him, tall as a man should be, his blue eyes unsure of what he was doing at her door. "Maybe we could talk or something."

"I'm not in the mood to talk."

"We could go out. What are you in the mood for?"

"Nothing."

"Come on."

She sighed. "Listen, I don't mean to be rude, but I have a night planned—a lava-hot shower, then an entire loaf of pound cake. And if I don't feel ill by then, a bag of those fire-hot Cheetos that turn your fingers red."

He smiled, and his dimples showed. "Wow."

"Yeah. I am wow. I'm also very tired and wet and…"

"And what?"

She sighed. "And nothing." She shook her head, then turned and opened her door. "I'll see you, Trent."

He caught her hand. Carrie stopped, stilled, listened to the sound of her heartbeat as it pounded against the walls of her chest. If his hand felt good, then…

She never got to finish the thought. Trent turned her around and pulled her against him. His arms went around her, crushing her breasts into the solid wall of his chest. She held her breath as she watched his head drop, felt his hair brush the side of her face, the stubble on his chin against her cheek.

She didn't move. She wanted to know what he had planned, what he was going to do next. He brushed her wet hair aside with his face and kissed that spot between her shoulder and neck. A soft, tame kiss, but for Carrie it was as though that spot were a dam, holding back every ounce of passion she'd been storing up. And when his mouth connected with that spot, the dam broke and the flood of feeling was unstoppable.

Her legs shook, and between them a hot, wet ache circled and teased her senses. She closed her eyes and tipped her chin up, welcomed his mouth on hers. His kiss was warm, soft and unhurried, and she melted into him, let him hold her up, care for her heavy limbs as he cared for her hungry mouth. It had been a long time since she felt cared for, a long time since anyone had carried her.

No one led the kiss. Each had their own style and each gave in to what the other wanted. Trent liked to nip at her lower lip, then suckle it before kissing her deeply. Carrie loved the feeling of his tongue in her mouth, just those soft playful swipes against her lips, teeth, tongue, as her hands played in his hair.

Then she felt Trent's hand on her naked belly, felt his fingers moving upward. She put her hand over his on the outside of her shirt, but instead of stopping him, she led him up to the spot where her heart pounded wildly in her chest.

She said quickly and without thought, "Do you want to come inside?"

He nodded. "Yes."

She smiled.

Then he said, "But I can't."

His words made her freeze, her heart drop into her throat. She swallowed painfully and looked up at him.

His jaw looked tight, as if he was really pissed but trying to hold it in. He eased his hand from her. "I have to go."

"What?"

"I have to go. Now."

She just stared at him, calling herself an idiot. A total masochistic idiot. What the hell had she expected from this guy? "Then please go," she said caustically. She turned around and muttered the word *jerk* as she stalked into her apartment.

Carrie was no drama queen, but on this night, she actually slammed the door. Then she proceeded to bolt it, turn her back on it and lean against it.

Okay.

Yes, she'd been a fool.

But she wasn't going to dwell.

She wasn't about to give in to an all-night chastise-fest. So, she'd kissed a cute guy. Big deal. It happened all the time—maybe not to her, but whatever. It had felt good, and now that she knew what she'd been missing, maybe she'd open herself up, ask someone out, go out on a date or two.

Trent Tanford—forgotten!

Then came a knock on her door, and her gut clenched and twisted.

Releasing the weighty breath she'd been holding, she turned around and opened the door, prepared herself to be civil.

Carrie stared expectantly at the man on the other side of the threshold.

"Please tell me you're not actually back for more?" she said, her tone dripping with sarcasm as she tried not to think about the horrific realization that if her body had a brain of its own it would walk straight for Trent Tanford and lock lips with him right now.

He leaned against the doorjamb, his blue eyes heavy with concern. "I'm such an ass."

For one brief second she thought of slamming the door in his face, but she was a New Yorker. Arguing and sarcastic potshots that masked sexual attraction were much more her style. She sighed. "Add a 'hole' onto that word and you got it just about right."

He laughed, shook his head. "Listen, I had a really bad day today."

"Yeah, I know about those."

He inclined his head. "I apologize."

Her anger slipped just a touch, and she nodded. "Apology accepted."

"Can I make it up to you?"

"Thanks, but I have everything I need."

"Pound cake and hot Cheetos?"

She paused, rewound what he'd just said in her mind and let her shoulders droop. "That sounded really pathetic when you said it."

He laughed. "I insist on making it up to you, Miss Gray."

"There's nothing to make up for. You don't have to do any—"

"Stop, please." He pushed away from the wall. He was just too good-looking. So tall, muscular, dimples and eyes blazing sex. He was breathtaking. He said softly, "I think you know enough about me, or my reputation, to know that I don't do anything because I have to."

"That's probably true, but—"

He took her hand then, and her legs threatened to buckle. His eyes were serious as he said, "I like you. Enough to stop things from going too far in the hallway of our apartment building." When she grinned, he followed. "There's something about you that fires me up, Carrie Gray, and not just in the sex department. I want to see you again."

Awareness moved through her, snaking through her belly, circling her breasts. "What do you have in mind?"

"Go out with me."

"When?"

"Friday night."

Her brows lifted. "A date?"

He nodded. "Seven-thirty." It wasn't a question.

Carrie attempted to toss in a little cold-water sanity. "I hate to say it, but I'm not your type, Trent."

He stared at her, then shook his head, grinned. "Maybe you are. Maybe it's about time that smart *and* beautiful was my type."

Well, then, Carrie mused. Sanity could go take a hike.

She smiled. "All right." Then she remembered that she would be coming from her mom's place. "Can we meet somewhere?"

"Sure. How about The Lexington Church?"

Her brows lifted. "A church?"

He paused a moment, looking just slightly sheepish. "There's something I need to tell you."

Oh God. What now? "You're a priest."

He grinned. "No."

"No," she muttered. "I didn't think so."

"It's actually something I need to ask you."

All of a sudden it felt as though a bag of bugs had been released under her shirt—a sensation that usually indicated that it would be a good time to run the other way.

"Carrie 12B Gray?"

"Yes…"

"This is going to sound completely insane."

"Not the best way to begin a question."

He dropped to one knee in front of her. "I've only known you for a day."

"Not much better, Trent."

"But I think you're the one."

The one? *Twilight Zone* music started to play in her head.

He grinned, flashing those damn dimples. "Will you marry me?"

Three

Stunned wasn't the word for it.

Freaked-out didn't quite cut it, either.

Maybe massively pissed off…?

It was like eighth grade all over again and Mr. Popular Hunk, Stuart Kaplan, had just brought an excited Carrie to the homecoming football game, where he proceeded to hold her hand, kiss her with too much tongue and parade her in front of all his friends. But not because he actually liked her. He was looking to mess with her, which he did by digging out the chewing tobacco from inside his lower lip and smashing it in her hair.

The feeling of that moment would live inside of her forever. Total foolishness, totally duped.

She tried to keep her voice even when she spoke to Trent. "I've been out of junior high for a long time now and I'm not into jock games."

He stood up. "What?"

She raised a brow at him. "You need to go home now."

"I know this sounds—"

"I'm going inside." She turned around and tried to close the door, but Trent stopped her.

"Carrie, wait a second."

"No."

"I'm the ass. Again. I was trying to make light of a really odd position that I find myself in. I really do like you. If you'd just let me explain—"

She shot him a venomous look. "Don't ever knock on my door again." Then she closed the door in his face.

This time she didn't lean against it feeling sad. She walked straight into the kitchen and to the freezer where her pound cake awaited.

She loved New York, but honest to God there were some serious nut jobs running free. And to think she'd been so attracted to him, had actually felt a connection to him, had seen a glimpse of what it would be like to have someone to share a bad day with….

That was, until his cruel side had surfaced.

"Rumors are buzzing around this place like flies in the horse stalls over in Riverdale where my sister goes for her riding lessons."

Trent looked up. Danny, the sandwich guy, stood in

the doorway, a lopsided grin on his round, freckled face. He was bold and unapologetic in the way he addressed the second in command of AMS, always was. And Trent allowed it, though he would never allow anyone else to speak to him that way. To Trent, the young man was entertaining, like a kid brother who was finding his way. A brother Trent had always wished he'd had.

No one in the office knew it, but Trent had been paying for Danny's college tuition for the past two years. The kid was really sharp and would make a killer attorney someday.

"I don't have time for gossip, Dan. You know that."

Danny closed the door and walked into the room. "Even when it's about you?"

"Especially when it's about me."

"All right, but if you do get married you're going to invite me, right?"

Trent frowned. "Don't you have class?"

"Not until two."

"Don't you have sandwiches to deliver?"

Danny grinned. "So, who is she?"

Trent was silent.

"Supermodel or actress?"

"You should get to class early. It shows commitment."

"It shows that I'm a serious nerd. But speaking of commitment…I can't believe you're getting married."

"Have a nice day, Dan."

Danny pointed to work on Trent's desk. "What are you doing there? Writing your vows?"

The look Trent shot Danny had him backing up toward the door with his hands up. "All right, all right."

When Danny was gone, Trent leaned back in his chair and looked over the information his P.I. had procured for him. Carrie Claudette Gray, aspiring graphic designer, house sitter for a prince, had attended public school and had been a great student. Got a job at an art gallery at the age of fourteen, was a candy striper and ESL instructor. Mom was an artist, Dad not in the picture. After high school, attended The School of Visual Arts in Manhattan. Boyfriends, marriages—none to speak of.

Interesting, Trent thought.

She was a good girl, that was for sure—an everywoman—but the best part of all was that she needed financial help. Massive school loans, a temporary position as a house sitter, and no graphic design job yet.

He turned around in his chair and stared out the window at the skyline. Could he actually do this? Be a married man? He'd gotten close once before, back in the idiot years between eighteen and twenty.

During college, he'd met a woman he'd thought was the love of his life. She was a gorgeous socialite, older, twenty-five, and had wanted to get married and have kids right away. A barely legal Trent had been so in love, he'd agreed. One week before the wedding, she'd called to say that she'd married someone else, and was at that exact moment on her honeymoon with him. She'd given no apology, just a quick explanation that the man she'd married had offered her a better life, a better deal.

Trent had been broken for a good year after that. Then he'd come to understand something: that maybe marriage was just a deal to be made and agreed upon when you were ready.

So, he mused, turning back to his desk, was he ready now? Could he make the deal for a short time to appease his father and take control of AMS?

Yes. Being head of AMS was worth a year in jail— especially if the jailer kissed like that.

He grabbed the phone, pushed a few buttons and when he had his father on the line, informed him that they had a deal.

Now all that was left to do was persuade the lady.

The Park Café was located on the corner of Seventy-first and Park and was attached to Trent's building. The spacious wi-fi hotspot was a popular place, especially during the two biggest lulls in brain activity: early morning and between four and five.

When Trent walked in during the latter, he spotted Carrie right away, sitting at a table with Elizabeth Wellington. Elizabeth lived in the penthouse with her husband, Reed, whom Trent had played ball with a few times. He didn't know them all that well, but they seemed happy enough.

As Trent approached the table, he noticed that the pretty redhead was crying as she talked animatedly to Carrie. He couldn't help but overhear a small part of the conversation.

"I've told him a hundred times, but you know Reed isn't the kind of man who'll take—"

Elizabeth spotted him then and immediately stopped talking. When she saw that he was coming over to the table, she leaned in and whispered something to Carrie then grabbed her purse and left the table. She didn't meet Trent's gaze as she pushed past him.

Carrie sat back in her chair, arms folded over her chest. "Trent Tanford, making women run away all over Manhattan."

He nodded. "Yes, I suppose I deserve that."

She took a sip of her coffee. "Are you here for coffee or just to eavesdrop?"

He sat down in the chair Elizabeth had vacated moments before. "I'm here to apologize."

"Already forgotten."

"Doesn't sound like it."

"No?"

He shook his head.

"Fine." She took a breath and said, "Apology heard and begrudgingly accepted then."

The corners of his mouth twitched with amusement. Damn, he really liked this woman. He'd never met anyone like her, anyone who made him smile this much.

"Listen," he began, "the marriage proposal—"

"Okay *that* one is forgotten. Seriously."

"The thing is, I'm not looking for you to forget the proposal—just the way it was delivered."

Before she could say another word or get up and

leave, he moved on. "I have a problem and I need your help. I'm *this* close to having everything I've ever wanted—the position at my company that I was meant to have, that I've worked my ass off to have. But to get it I need to—" he lifted a brow "—be married."

She stared at him for a second, then muttered a terse "Jeez." She stood up and grabbed her coffee. "I'm out of here."

"Carrie, wait." He went after her.

"You need mental help."

"Maybe so, but not for this."

She walked past him and headed for the elevator.

"Where are you going? I need to talk to you."

When he followed her into the elevator and pressed the button for their floor, Carrie whirled on him with her best "I'm-an-ass-kicker" face, her finger jabbing him in the chest. "Look, I get that you're mister high-profile-make-a-lot-of-money-so-I-can-impress-the-women-then-play-mind-games-with-them-stud-wannabe."

"Wow," he muttered, "that was a mouthful."

"And I'm sure there are a boatload of women in this city who are totally into that, but I'm not one of them."

Trent decided to ease up on the back and forth, tit-for-tat play. No matter how fun it was to watch his soon-to-be bride get all fired up, he didn't have a lot of time. He leaned forward and stopped the elevator.

They both jerked forward. Carrie sucked in a breath. "What the hell do you think you're doing?"

"You talk a lot."

"So do you."

"That wasn't an insult. I like it. I love watching your mouth move, and I look forward to watching it in the future, but right now I need you to listen."

Her jaw tightened and her tone was menacing. "You need to move and let me start this elevator back up or I'm going to scream."

"I know your situation."

"What situation?"

"Your financial situation."

She grew still. She swallowed and said with a lack of confidence he'd never seen before, "What?"

"Listen, I had to do what I had to do."

"You had me checked out?"

He shrugged nonchalantly. "Purely professional. If you're going to become a Tanford I had to know about your background."

She threw her hands in the air. "I'm not becoming a Tanford! In fact, right now, the idea of punching a Tanford sounds way more satisfying than marrying one."

"I think we're going to be good together. I need someone who will push me."

"You're delusional." She punched the emergency button and they went sailing upward.

He turned serious. "Marry me, Carrie. Stay married to me for one year and in return I will right all of your debt and kick in five hundred grand."

The doors opened.

He continued, "I'm sure there is something important you could do with that money."

"Goodbye, Trent."

"An apartment of your own."

She ignored him.

"Someone you could help," he called after her.

She paused, halfway down the hall. Didn't move for one whole minute. Then she shook her head and kept walking until she disappeared inside her apartment.

Four

Rachel Gray had been an amazing single mother. Yes, she'd worked night and day and all the hours in between on her artwork. But even so, Carrie had never felt unloved or neglected. Quite the opposite, in fact. Rachel had always found a way to involve her daughter in her work, setting up a canvas beside her own for Carrie or having her mix paints or letting her go nuts with color on one wall of the living room. And when Rachel wasn't working, life was boldly interesting and fun— a dark kind of fun, like waking Carrie up in the middle of the night with several rolls of toilet paper stuffed under her flannel pajama top, and a sly grin on her face.

"Let's go up to the roof deck, give the trees a little white. Pretend it's Christmas."

Carrie closed the prince's high-tech stainless-steel refrigerator door and smiled as she remembered that night. Yesterday and today, she was proud to have such a mother, and she knew that Rachel was proud of her, as well.

She took a breath. Would her mother be proud of a daughter who sold herself for money?

Carrie poured herself a glass of orange juice. Times had changed since those days when Rachel was a full-time painter, free to live life the way she wanted, in control of her thoughts and memories. These days Rachel needed her rent covered, her meals paid for and full-time care, and her daughter was barely making it.

Carrie drank the entire glass of juice, then headed into her room to change out of her best business suit. She needed to keep it in perfect condition for the next interview, because the meeting she'd had this morning was a no-go. Not enough experience. She'd heard it five times in the past month.

The problem was, she kept trying for high-level positions in graphic design, ones that paid high-level salaries. Unfortunately, she didn't have the experience they required. She was just hoping that someone might look past the experience and see her talent and drive, and give her a chance, because an entry-level job was not going to pay her enough.

The bed dipped with her weight. She slipped off her

shoes. She wouldn't go there, not a chance. This insane idea of Trent's.

She took off her stockings.

How could someone even suggest being married for a year? Basically, a business arrangement.

No sex, just for show.

Well. She paused. She was assuming there'd be no sex. But she should never assume—especially when it came to Trent Tanford.

A shiver of awareness moved through her at the unbidden image of lying in Trent's bed as he took off his clothes and stood before her, hovered over her, every inch of him lean and hard and ready to please. Trent Tanford taking off her shoes, her stockings…

Carrie leaned forward, put her head between her knees and tried to breathe.

Her school loans would be a thing of the past. She could actually afford to take an entry-level position at a graphic design house, really work her way up, take the time to learn without worrying about her mother's financial situation. And in the future be able to afford to care for Rachel long term.

The phone rang and Carrie leaped for it, hoping it was Trent calling to beg her to reconsider.

But it wasn't.

"Hey, Tessa." Carrie kept her voice light as she spoke to Prince Sebastian's personal assistant. "How are things?"

"Good, good." Tessa paused for a second and Carrie could just imagine the pretty green-eyed blonde sitting at her desk, which was, as usual, dutifully organized. "I have some news. Prince Sebastian is going to be returning soon."

"Is everything all right?"

"Nothing major." Tessa Banks was never one to gossip, but Carrie sensed something in her tone, a concern for her boss that had never been there before. Of course, Carrie could've been misreading the situation.

"Tessa?"

The woman didn't say anything for a moment, then she sighed. "There's a little trouble with the company."

"Is Sebastian okay?"

"You know the prince. He's not happy if things aren't going according to plan."

"Yes, I do know." Sebastian Stone was a good man, but he was also a demanding boss who showed his dark moods from time to time.

"I'll call you a few days before his flight," Tessa continued, "and I'll make sure your standard room at the Mercer is booked."

While Carrie appreciated Sebastian Stone's thoughtfulness in making sure she had a place to stay while he was in town, living in a hotel was a lonely existence. She wondered again if she should stay with her mother. But there was really no room, and she didn't want to take any space away from Wanda, who was there a good deal of the time. "Do you know how long the prince will be in town?"

"I don't, sorry."

"No problem. Thanks, Tessa."

Carrie hung up the phone and for a good sixty seconds just sat there on the bed, still and silent. Then without another thought, she grabbed a pen and paper off the bedside table. In a calm hand she wrote a brief note, then she snatched up her house keys and left the apartment.

She couldn't do this face-to-face. If she did, she'd probably choke and back out.

Her heart slammed against her chest as she bent down in front of his door and slipped the note underneath.

At precisely 7:00 a.m. the following morning, Trent walked into the Park Café, his gaze raking every table in an almost predatory way. Then he spotted her. She was sitting by herself at a table near the bathroom, staring into her coffee and biting her lip. She was nervous. Trent wondered why. What did she have to say to him? After all, she hadn't given him a definitive answer in her note, just a request to meet her at the café.

Trent maneuvered past the tables; fat, comfortable couches; and a long line of thirsty patrons. He had been only partly surprised to hear from her again. Was she going to accept his offer?

A flash of heat moved through him, not sexual heat, but something altogether unfamiliar to him, something akin to possessiveness. Like an animal, beating its chest and howling. *She was his.* The fierceness of his reaction startled the hell out of him, and as he approached her table, he told himself that it was due to his desperate need to get this done, make this match happen, procure the position as head of AMS, and not a desperate need to have her.

He didn't sit down. "Do I have time to order an espresso, or is this going to be half a cup of the house blend kind of conversation?"

Carrie took a deep breath, then said matter-of-factly, "I'm going to take the deal."

"The deal?" He knew exactly what she meant.

She looked down her lovely nose at him and said tightly, "Marrying you, for the one year."

He nodded. "Good."

She nodded. "Good."

He turned then and waved to the barista, who knew him well and would slip his espresso order in right away despite the line.

Trent knew he appeared calm as he sat down beside her, but inside him a fierceness raged, a satisfaction at getting what he most desired. She was his. She was his for one year. And so was AMS.

He watched her drink her coffee, which was no doubt cold at this point. Though she was without her glasses, she looked the same as she always did: cute, petite and casually dressed in jeans and a black peasant shirt. But as his gaze moved from the top of her head downward, he realized that every inch of her seemed to glow. Her long, dark hair, which was pulled back off her face to reveal those intense, probing, green eyes. And the full, pouty lips that he could still taste. And the curves.

Every damn inch of her glowed under his gaze.

The barista came over and set a double espresso before him, then flashed him her sexiest smile.

He hardly noticed. "Thanks," he muttered.

The woman in front of him was still glowing.

Completely fixed on Carrie, Trent couldn't help the words that tumbled out of his mouth then, like crude stones into a polisher. "I know I suggested that this marriage be a business arrangement, but you should know that I find you incredibly attractive. I don't know how easy it will be for me not to touch you, kiss you again, but if you don't want to go there—"

"I don't."

Her quick rebuff wounded Trent's healthy ego, but he didn't show it. He shrugged. "All right. I can respect that."

"Good." She was quick to add, "But I'll understand if you want to find…that—"

"That?"

"Sex." She whispered the word as though they were in church and not a coffeehouse brimming with groups of people talking and laughing and using their cell phones.

He couldn't help grinning. "Right."

"If you want to find it elsewhere."

His grin remained. "Thank you."

She nodded succinctly. "You're welcome."

Trent watched her expression, her pink cheeks and the unmasked sexual curiosity in her eyes. He was no fool. Carrie Gray liked him, quite a lot if he wasn't mistaken. And whatever her reasons were that day for sticking up the No Trespassing sign, Trent was pretty confident he could get her to remove it in short order.

"You know," he began evenly, "it's been my experience that women don't appreciate sharing their husbands."

"I'm sure that's true." Her green eyes flashed as she stared over her coffee cup at him. "But you won't be my husband—not in any real sense."

Again, that uncontrolled pull of possession moved over him. He lifted his cup and sipped his espresso, the hot liquid doing its best to calm this new, unchecked beast within. "Listen, Carrie, even though you're cool with me getting my pleasure on the side, I'm afraid I can't allow you the same privilege."

He'd never seen anyone sit up in their seat that quickly before. "Allow me?" She repeated his words with slow gall.

"That's right."

"I don't follow orders, Trent."

"Just think of it as part of the deal."

"You can't just add anything you want to this deal anytime you want."

"We are going to be married for one year. Looking for sex outside of our marriage would be humiliating and damaging to both our reputations." He put down his cup and leveled a serious gaze at her. "I swear right here and right now that I will not break my marriage vow to you."

She stared at him, disbelieving. "No other women?"

"That's right. For one year no other woman but my wife."

She swallowed as she registered what he'd said. Then she smiled just a hint of a smile. "So, you're going to be celibate for one year, huh? Do you really think you can do that?"

No. He didn't think so. Especially with her walking around his apartment night and day, bathing in his tub, sitting beside him on the couch, glowing the whole damn time.

Trent took a swallow of his coffee and hissed through his teeth.

"What?" she asked, her concern not lost on him. "Too hot?"

He stared at her. "Could be. Could very well be."

They got married the following Saturday in a rushed affair by elite caterer, Abigail Kirsch, at The Lighthouse at Chelsea Piers. A wonderful location, but far too large a space for their small party, and only managed because of who the Tanfords were in New York society, and who they knew.

No rings and a nontraditional ceremony had been Carrie's two major requests from Trent. Since girlhood, she'd dreamed of the perfect ring and being married in a church. But since this was not the "real" wedding she'd always imagined, she had insisted that she and Trent exchange vows without the platinum and in a location that was totally untraditional—yet public and fabulous enough so that Trent's father would be assured the affair would wind up in the papers.

Which it had, along with James Tanford's imminent retirement from AMS.

Carrie wore a sweet, insanely expensive Amsale dress that had been selected for her by the wedding coordinator working for the Tanfords. She even wore her hair the way the woman had suggested. She felt that, after all, this wasn't "her" wedding, so what did it matter?

All the guests were Tanford guests, of course, as Carrie hadn't invited her mother or any of her friends. She had planned to tell them that her and Trent's wedding had been a whirlwind decision and quickly executed, much like an elopement. But she knew there would be questions, uncomfortable questions, coming her way.

At 4:00 p.m. Saturday afternoon, she stood with Trent, who looked unbearably handsome in a black tuxedo, in front of floor-to-ceiling windows that overlooked the Hudson River. With his guests and stoic family behind them, Carrie and Trent agreed to be married. Afterward, Carrie spoke to his mother and father, who were poised and tall, and seemed genuinely pleased by the match. But they were also as affectionally retarded as most of the extremely wealthy couples she'd met in Manhattan, and quickly opted out of hugging either Carrie or their son.

There was music and an amazing spread, but Carrie ate little. As she walked around the party with Trent, she felt uneasy, lonely. The only thing familiar—the only thing that had warmed her on that incredibly warm late afternoon in August—was Trent's kiss, and the fact that his hand had never left hers since the ceremony had ended.

And then it was over. At seven o'clock they drove home, and with that kiss still lingering in her mind, Carrie wondered what was next, what about tomorrow—and how was she going to face being Mrs. Trent Tanford in name only?

Five

Carrie spent her wedding night in the most romantic of ways—packing up her belongings and moving out of Prince Sebastian's European-style apartment. As Sebastian was coming back to Manhattan soon anyway, she had called him earlier in the week to put in her resignation. He was sorry to lose her, he'd said, but understood her need to move on. Carrie hadn't told him what she was moving on to, but had assured him she would look after his place until his arrival, as promised.

"Ready?"

Trent stood in the bedroom doorway, looking ready to work. He had abandoned his tux for a much more casual ensemble of faded jeans and a funky black argyle

T-shirt with sleeves. When Carrie nodded, the two of them left the Old World of Europe and walked down the hall to a modern two-bedroom ultramasculine bachelor pad.

Trent's place had a very similar layout to the prince's apartment, but the paint choices, decor and "toys" were totally different. There was modern art and framed photographs on the gray walls, most of which were shot in and around New York City in a photojournalistic style. A flat-screen TV sat above the white brick fireplace in the living area, and around the metal-and-glass coffee table were modern black leather and metal couches. Behind that, near one of the windows, was an area that seemed to be designated for relaxation with a high-tech massage chair, surround sound stereo and DVD player, and some other male-oriented gadgets she didn't recognize.

On the way to her new room, they passed by his kitchen, which was open and airy, and looked brand-new, with granite countertops, electric-blue tile backsplash and expensive stainless steel appliances. Carrie grinned and shook her head when she saw dishes piled up in the sink.

He might be a rich guy, but Trent Tanford was a guy nonetheless.

Trent carried her bags into a good-size room that was painted the color of sand and boasted a white oak dresser with stainless steel legs and a metallic gray ceiling fan with wide leaves. Below the fan sat a modern queen-size bed with a creamy-colored upholstered headboard, metal legs and lots of plump white bedding. Two metal side tables held up two modern white lamps. Carrie noticed the short, wide vases on each table that were filled with red roses, cut short and packed closely together.

It was a beautiful room.

Trent set down her bags. "This used to be my office, but I think it'll be much better with you in it."

Her heart moved with the compliment. Very sweet. She looked over her shoulder at him. "That's a nice thing to say."

He raised a brow. "I have more nice things."

She smiled. "I'm sorry about taking your office away from you."

"No problem. But if you feel really bad about it, you can always move into my room and I'll put the desk and computers back in here."

"How about I just say thanks and leave it at that?" He was damn charming, she'd give him that. Resisting him would be difficult, but she had to. If she didn't, what would that make her? His for a year, and then done, out of his life—paid in full.

The idea made her cringe.

Perhaps sensing her discomfort, Trent continued with the tour. He moved beside her and pointed to the door at his right, which was bracketed by two framed photographs of old, paint-crackled window frames. "This room has its own bathroom. There are fresh towels in there, and I had Hannah, my housekeeper, get you a robe and a few…girl things."

"Girl things?" she repeated.

He looked at her and laughed. It was an infectious sound. "I don't know. Come on, give me a break. You are my first true houseguest, Carrie."

"Yeah, right."

"Believe it or not."

"You know which one I'm going with. I used to guide the poor lost lambs over here, remember?"

He walked over to her, his gaze serious. "I had women here, true. But no one stayed past 7:00 a.m."

She was appalled by his honesty. "That's horrible."

"Maybe so, but it was understood."

She raised her brows, unable to speak.

"I am who I am, Carrie. I set up my life the way I wanted it, and whoever decided to come into that life had a choice."

She nodded. "Okay. Fine, I get that. But why nothing after 7:00 a.m.?"

He shrugged. "It sends the wrong message."

"And what is that exactly? I don't like people who sleep late or eat breakfast?"

"No. More like, I don't want you thinking that this is anything more than a few hours of fun."

Her brow lifted. "Breakfast is too intimate?"

"Exactly."

"Talking about what could be next over pancakes and eggs…"

"I'm an honest man. No one came into this house without that knowledge."

"Gotcha."

"Yes, you do." It happened in a flash. He took her hand and brought it to his mouth. "For one year." Then he turned her hand over and kissed the palm.

Carrie's knees nearly gave out as heat traveled up her wrist, into her arm, shoulders.... He had an amazing mouth, gentle and full, teasing her with his slow, deliberate movements.

And then she remembered herself and eased her hand away from him. "I'm going to unpack now."

"And I'm going to let you," he said evenly, though his gaze was heavy with heat.

He was halfway out the door when Carrie called to him, "This is a crazy thing we're doing here."

In the doorway, he stopped and turned. "What? The marriage or the attraction thing?"

Her eyes went wide. "Yes."

He laughed. "You don't do too many crazy things, do you, Carrie?"

She shook her head. "No. Not really."

"Well, just so you know, the level of crazy is entirely up to you."

Perfect, she thought darkly. Leave the decision of how much water to drink to a chick who was dying of thirst. Smart move, Park Avenue Boy!

"I'm going to make some dinner," he said, "After you unpack, you're welcome to join me."

She wanted to say yes. She really did. But she needed some time to think, figure out her next move, the plan for this year-long "marriage." So she shook her head.

"I'm really tired. It's been a long day."

He looked disappointed, but he didn't push. He said, "Well, good night," then closed the door.

And she was alone again.

Releasing a heavy breath, Carrie sat on the bed in her black "wedding night" sweats and stared out the window at her new view, ignoring the grumble in her belly and the heat that still smoldered just inches below it.

It was a dream.

She knew it was a dream. She just didn't want to wake up and have it end. Her body felt like liquid metal, cool, smooth, pliable, the way it moved under his. But her insides, in contrast, her muscles, bones and blood all erupted in a blaze of heat.

"Carrie?"

The soft sound of her name wasn't coming from his mouth, the mouth poised above hers. Although the voice was his.

"Carrie?"

And then he was gone in a flash of white and she could feel the sheets against her back and her hair on her face. She opened her eyes. Trent was standing over her looking like the cover of a magazine. Suit, tie, clean shaven, eyes as blue as faded denim.

Yummy, was all she could think.

"What time is it?"

"Seven," he told her. "I'm sorry about coming in here and waking you up, but I didn't want to leave without saying goodbye. I thought it would be strange for you to wake up and… Well, a note seemed…"

"Right." It was thoughtful of him and she gave him a smile. "Thanks."

From her spot, deep within the white swell of covers, she caught a trace of his aftershave, and the clean, ocean scent made her already shaky, swollen, desire-filled body respond.

If she reached up and grabbed the lapels of his fancy, custom-made suit, pulled him down on top of her and kissed him, what would he do? What would he think of her? What would she think of herself? She'd just married the man yesterday, just stuffed her boxed wedding dress into his "office" closet, just made a pact with herself not to get physical with him.

Then another scent caught her attention, something earthier. Nuts or coffee? She looked to her right and saw coffee, toast and some fruit on her bedside table.

She looked at him, her eyebrows lifted. "That looks like breakfast, Trent."

He grinned. "Yes, I suppose it does."

"What happened to your rule?"

"Those rules we discussed last night don't apply to you or to us."

She felt the wave of happiness move through her, and wished it would never go away. "You're trying really hard, aren't you?" she said.

"What do you mean?"

"To be a good husband."

He grinned. "I've always been an overachiever."

"Well, you've definitely made me feel welcome here." She sat up, knowing full well that her hair was all over the place but not caring at that moment. "So, do you have to go right this second?"

Beside her, she felt Trent's body tense. "Why?"

She took a sip of coffee. "That comment you made last night about me and my lack of craziness…"

"Yes?"

"I think it's time to get a little crazy."

"And how exactly do you plan to do that?"

With a grin, she pointed to the plate beside the bed. "You made this for me, so how about you can feed it to me."

Trent laughed, his whole body relaxing. "I like you, you know that? I like you a lot." He reached over and picked up the white plate. "Here you go." He slipped a lovely blackberry into her open mouth.

When she closed her mouth and smiled at him, he shook his head and muttered, "Damn you."

They both laughed, and Trent continued feeding her until every blackberry was gone.

"Thank you for this," she said sipping her coffee. "Seriously. It's really nice."

"I meant what I said in the Park Café, Carrie. You're the only one."

As her heart expanded at his words, Carrie couldn't help but wonder why this major player in the dating world was so focused on her, why he was being such a kind, considerate husband-type. Was it simply because he honored the vow they'd taken? Or was it something else?

But then he leaned in close to her mouth and whispered, "You're the only one…okay?" She forgot everything she'd just been thinking and she closed her eyes and whispered back, "Okay."

And then he kissed her. And she let him.

First he kissed her mouth, so softly, then her chin, both cheeks, her eyes, her earlobes, then her mouth once more.

It was nothing charged or intensely sexual, but everything south of Carrie's belly ached, pulsed, begged for him to continue.

Where were his hands? His fingers?

But when she opened her eyes, he had backed up, his own gaze looking strained.

"I have to go," he said.

"I know," she said.

"Dinner tonight?"

"I'll cook," she said, then smiled at him. "And I'll feed."

He inhaled sharply and looked away. "You are a devious, torturous woman, Carrie Tanford."

It was as if someone had wrapped a hot towel around her and squeezed. Carrie Tanford. It sounded too strange, wrong, yet she wanted to hear him say it again.

He saw her reaction and he smiled, stopped her before she could say anything. "I'll be home around eight."

When he was gone, Carrie leaned back in her bed and groaned. She was frustrated and unfulfilled, her appetite raging desperately for the man she had married—the man she had vowed not to touch.

Trent was on top of the world.

At one-thirty that afternoon, in conference room C, with every top AMS executive seated around the oval mahogany table, James Tanford had announced his retirement, effective immediately. Taking over as chairman and CEO would be his son, Trent Tanford. No one seemed shocked by this news; they had known it would happen eventually. But for Trent, hearing his father say the words had made his life infinitely sweeter.

After his father's announcement, Trent announced who would be stepping into his previous position and subsequent other positions down the line, before unveiling his plan to rocket AMS into first place in the ever-present media wars before the year's end.

By seven-thirty that evening, he was happily exhausted and ready to head home, to his wife.

With a confident grin on his face, he walked out of the AMS building into the hot August night. His company car sat outside waiting for him, the black paint gleaming in the fading sunset.

His driver, Michael, stood sentry at the door and nodded as Trent approached. "Good evening, sir."

Trent agreed jovially, "Very good."

"Yes, sir."

Michael opened the door and Trent climbed into the

backseat, where the surprise of a lifetime sat directly across from him.

"Carrie. What the—"

"Hi."

She smiled at him in a warm, soft way that made his insides twist with desire. "Hey."

She looked different, though very much like herself in manner and realness. But there had been a definite change. Gone were the jeans, the peasant tops and dresses—all very good things, he mused, but nothing like what was before him. He'd known she had amazing curves, but he'd never seen them before, not like this.

His mouth watered as his gaze moved over her, starting with her feet and the metallic high-heeled sandals that showed off ten beautifully painted toes. Her legs were bare, but mostly covered by a long scarlet-colored strapless dress that hugged her curves and displayed her large full breasts to his hungry gaze.

Trent's only thought in that moment was to flip up the privacy partition and feast on her.

He was so turned-on he could barely talk, barely hear anything going on outside the car or in. But through the buzzing sound of his body in heat, he heard her say, "Do you want to know why I'm here?"

"Yes," he uttered.

"I thought I'd take you to dinner."

"You did?"

"To celebrate."

He stared at her, at her beautiful face that required

so little makeup, at her long dark hair that hung loose about her shoulders.

She laughed at him. "Your big day, Trent."

"What?"

"Weren't you promoted today? The job you've been working for all your life. Any of this ringing a bell?"

He found his way back to reality and nodded. "Right. Of course. I'm just…"

"Just what?"

Yes, what was he? Desperate? Overwhelmed by her? What was he exactly?

In the end, he came up with, "Surprised."

"Well, good." She looked past him. "To Babbo please, Michael."

"Very good, ma'am."

Carrie turned back to Trent. "And just a few short days ago, I was a 'miss.'"

"You look stunning."

She blushed, full on. She looked down, then back up at him. "Thank you."

How he was ever going to go home with her and not touch her was beyond him. What an asinine promise he'd given her—going at her pace or not at all! What a jerk! He leaned back against the black leather. "What if I said to hell with dinner?"

"Then I think we'd be having our first big fight."

"I don't want that."

"Me, either."

He smiled at her. "This is really nice of you."

She smiled back. "I, too, am an overachiever. And a good friend to have."

His smile fell at the friend comment, but he caught himself quickly, and when they pulled up to the restaurant a few minutes later, he had forced himself back into a good mood.

Before she got out, Trent said, "You know that once we step foot in that restaurant you're going to be scrutinized."

"Head to toe?"

"Soup to nuts."

"They'll want to know everything about Trent Tanford's new bride?"

"Yes," he said, stepping out of the car and offering her his hand. "And honestly, who could blame them?"

She smiled at him, took his hand and let him help her out onto the stained, garbage-scented, but ever-magical New York City sidewalk.

They walked hand in hand into one of Manhattan's finest Italian restaurants.

Six

"Stop! Thief!"

Seated at the dining room table, Carrie glanced up from her work. It was ten o'clock and they'd returned from the restaurant about thirty minutes ago. Trent had jumped in the shower and Carrie had jumped into her job search.

Wearing a navy blue robe, Trent walked into the kitchen, his dark hair still wet. "Is that *my* takeaway bag from the restaurant?"

She looked down at her work again, because avoiding the beautiful man in the robe and bare feet sounded like a smart idea. "When did they start calling it that?" she said. "Takeaway bag? What happened to doggie bag?"

"I have no idea. Are you avoiding my question?"

"What question is that?"

Beer in hand, he came to sit beside her at the table. "Where is *your* doggie bag?"

"It's still in the fridge. Didn't you see it there?"

He chuckled, shook his head.

"Look, Trent," she began with mock seriousness, "let's be real here. You are way too cultured, way too chichi to eat leftovers, and you know it."

"That is so not true."

"Which part?"

"I am not chichi." He tipped his beer at her. "Want some?"

"Sure, why not." After a healthy swallow with Trent watching her the entire time, Carrie handed the bottle back to him and returned to her work.

"So, what are you doing here?" he asked.

"Rewriting my résumé."

"Need any help?"

"No. Thanks." He smelled so good, like man soap, musky and off-limits. She tried to breathe through her mouth instead of her nose, which was no easy feat. It sure would've helped to have a clothespin or something. "It's just a matter of making my few qualifications in the graphic design world sound more substantial than they really are."

"Let me see."

He took the paper.

Carrie sat up tall at the table, as though she were

interviewing for a position right then and there. "I am determined to get a real design job by the fall," she said as he studied it. "Entry level is fine, but I really want it to be with a top company. I want to learn from the best of the best."

He gave the résumé back to her and declared, "I know what you need to do to fix this."

"What?" she said, seizing his beer from him and taking a sip.

"You need to change your last name."

"What?"

"Change your last name to Tanford and you won't have a problem finding a job."

She looked shocked. "I can't do that."

"Why the hell not?"

She sat back in her chair and folded her arms over her chest protectively. "I want to get this job on my own merits."

"An employer won't take the time to look at your merits, Carrie." He leaned back in his chair, too, and drank his beer. "Do you know how many people are vying for graphic design jobs in Manhattan? And not the gofer type of job where in between shuffling papers, you're getting coffee and sandwiches for the partners."

She played with her nails. "I'm sure it's a lot."

"Thousands." He put down his beer and took her hand, the one she was playing with, and she looked up at him. "A headhunter will never even read your résumé unless something on it attracts their attention."

"Like the Tanford name."

He nodded. "Exactly."

"But there is more than one Tanford in this city."

"Not Carrie Tanford. Everyone in this city knows I got married, and who I married."

She sighed. "I don't know."

"It's not a bad name."

He looked like a proud little boy just then and she smiled at him. "No, it isn't." What was stopping her? What was it that made her cringe? The fact that she'd only have the name for a year? That it didn't really belong to her?

She was becoming a confused person. She didn't like being confused, not knowing her own feelings, what choice felt right.

The truth was, the more she was around this man, the more confused she became.

"Get the job, Carrie, then show them those merits of yours."

"They're good merits," she insisted, more to herself than to him.

"Very good," he agreed. "Very attractive merits that no company, no one, could turn down."

They were becoming fast friends, she and Trent. She could feel the warmth and familiarity of a growing bond between them. And that was fine, lovely. What concerned her was the undeniable attraction that circled that friendship. And it wasn't just the proximity, though that surely helped the attraction along. No, she'd felt this pull to him on the very first day they'd talked, at his door when she'd reamed him out about his misdirected newspaper and assorted girlfriends.

She took another swig of his beer and looked over her résumé again. She was, after all, Carrie Tanford, Mrs. Trent Tanford. What was the harm? She was a hard worker, a fast learner. She'd be an asset to any company that had the good sense to hire her.

She dropped the résumé on the table and declared, "All right, then. I'll do it."

"Good."

Trent leaned in and kissed her. It was a warm, possessive kiss, one that spoke volumes about what he wanted to do next.

When he pulled back, their mouths were just an inch or two apart. Carrie's heart pounded in her throat and she waited to see what he was going to do.

She wet her upper lip with her tongue.

Then he reached for her, lifted her onto his lap, his mouth searching for hers. Her arms went around his neck, and as she kissed him back she felt his erection press into her backside. She sighed into his mouth. Her body was not her own, or maybe it was just disconnected from her brain. Whatever it was, this was a lost cause. She couldn't resist her own desires anymore. She would just have to deal with the aftereffects when they came.

For now she was going to enjoy herself.

Sick of sitting sideways, she eased one leg over his lap so she was straddling him. His robe opened at the waist, revealing no underwear, just hot, hard, ready flesh, and she dropped down on top of him. His hands raked up her back as his mouth teased hers, changing angles, tongues gently and seductively teasing each other.

Then his hand was at the top of her scarlet dress, easing down one side, exposing her heavy breast to the coolness of the air-conditioned room. Carrie's breath hitched in her throat as Trent lowered his head and lapped hungrily at her nipple. He cupped her breast from underneath, pulled her gently into his mouth, suckled hard as she muttered, "Yes, right there. Stay there."

It was no shock that her panties were wet, and her core ached with a desire she couldn't recall ever knowing before. She wanted Trent in an almost painful way, wanted that rock-hard erection that pulsed against her to be pulsing inside her body.

Neither heard the knock at the door. Not right away anyway. But whoever was there was insistent, and their knock grew louder and more obnoxious with every heavy breath that Carrie and Trent expelled.

Trent cursed and eased back, his eyes unfocused like a drunken man.

"It's eleven o'clock at night," Carrie uttered.

Out in the hallway, they heard the sounds of their very eccentric neighbor's dogs barking, and a high-pitched female voice.

Carrie sighed. "That better not be Vivian Vannick-Smythe."

Trent cupped Carrie's face. "I'll be right back." Then he righted his robe and went to the door.

Carrie sat at the table, groggy and turned-on to the point of wanting to cry if she didn't get to have Trent in her bed tonight. But through her haze, she heard a disturbing sound—a woman's voice, high and persistent, and then Trent's low voice, impatient and annoyed.

Like a possessed animal, a very female animal, she got up, made sure her dress wasn't exposing any of her female bits and walked into the hallway. Trent was just closing the door.

"The past has come calling," he managed to say to her before there was another knock on the door, followed by a female whine. "Trent, please."

Trent shook his head at Carrie. "I'm so sorry. I don't know how she got in here. She saw us at Babbo tonight and is having some issues."

He turned, opened the door again. This time his voice was calm, sympathetic when he addressed her. "Madeline, go home."

The tall, thin, spectacular-looking redhead shook her head and pouted. "No."

"I'll call you a cab."

"I don't want a cab. What I want is for you to tell me why you would drag that little nothing through Babbo and call her your wife."

Okay, Carrie thought. *Little thing coming through.* She pushed past Trent.

"Carrie, wait," he began.

"It's okay. It's a woman thing." Carrie faced the stunning, yet slightly wasted model at the door and thought that maybe she was indeed a little thing because she actually had to look up the woman, who had to be a good six inches taller than herself. "Hi, Madeline."

The woman looked stunned to see Carrie there, but she recovered quickly. "So you're the one who claims to have married him?"

"Yes, I am," Carrie said calmly. "And you're the very tall, very beautiful person who has had too much to drink and is knocking on a man's door at eleven o'clock at night. Think about that."

Madeline's perfectly arched eyebrows knit together.

Carrie continued in a soft, gentle way, "Doesn't that seem a little too desperate for a woman like you? I mean, look at you."

Madeline swallowed, her pale brown eyes wide. "Yeah. Yeah, it does."

"Go home, take a bath, wake up tomorrow and begin again." Carrie reached out and touched her shoulder. "This is Manhattan, honey, there are moderately handsome, emotionally unavailable millionaires around every corner."

She smiled and nodded vigorously. "You're right. You're right. Thank you…?"

"Carrie," she supplied quickly.

"Thanks, Carrie."

"Can we call you a cab?"

She shook her head. "The doorman will do that. He adores me. Too bad he's only a doorman."

Carrie nodded sympathetically. "I know. Good night."

When Carrie closed the door, she turned to find Trent staring at her, his mouth open, utter astonishment on his face.

She shook her head at him. "I cannot believe it."

"I know. Again, I'm so sorry—"

"I cannot believe that one of your former bimbos actually found her way to your door without help."

He stared at her, then a wide grin broke out on his face, exposing those killer dimples. She smiled, too, and before long they were both laughing.

After a minute, after her laughing eased, Carrie walked past Trent and gave him a pat on the shoulder. "'Night, husband."

"Wait."

She turned. "What?"

It passed between them, the question of should they go there again, finish what they'd started before the Calvin Klein model had knocked on the door and sobered them both with her drunken ramblings.

Carrie answered for both of them with a tight smile and a slow shake of her head.

He nodded, clearly disappointed. "Okay."

"'Night."

"Carrie?"

"Yeah?"

He lifted a brow. "When you said, 'moderately handsome millionaire,' were you talking about me?"

"'Night, Trent." She grinned, then turned and headed

into her room, hearing him toss back a gruff and highly insecure, "You were just saying that to get rid of her, right?"

"I got a job!" Carrie announced a few days later as she sashayed into the apartment with the air of a person who had finally been accepted into an ultraexclusive sorority. "I just picked up the message on my cell phone. I'm so jazzed."

Trent was in the kitchen making dinner. When she rounded the corner and spied him at the island rolling sushi, he looked up and grinned. "Congratulations."

She inclined her head regally. "Thank you."

He looked good. He'd abandoned his suit for the day and was dressed casually in a pair of faded jeans and a pale blue T-shirt that accentuated his lightly tanned skin and fell just perfectly over his toned stomach, chest and shoulders.

"So, who's the lucky company?" he asked, handing her a glass of white wine.

"Ebett and Gregg."

His brows lifted. "Nice. Very nice." He tipped his own glass at her. "Cheers."

"Back atcha." As she sipped the dry Chardonnay, she studied him. "Wait a second."

"What?"

She walked over to him. "Why don't you seem surprised about this?"

"Did you put Tanford on the résumé?"

"Yes."

He lifted his eyebrows and gestured with his hands, as if to say, "That's why."

She slugged him playfully on the shoulder. "Smarty-pants."

He slipped his hands around her waist and pulled her against him. "That's what they call me."

"Really?" she said, her heart thudding in her chest. "They call you that? Around the office and everything?"

"Mmm-hmm."

"So, when your assistant ushers all the top execs into your office, she says, 'Here they are for your two o'clock meeting, Smarty-Pants.'"

With a grin, Trent leaned in and whispered in her ear, "Maybe I should be calling you smarty-pants."

She laughed, then sighed as he kissed her neck. "Smarty-Ass may be more appropriate here."

He growled against her skin, then pushed her away gently. "Go in and check out your closet."

"Why?" She liked being close to him, the weight of him, the warmth of his skin against hers.

"Just do it," he ordered.

She rolled her eyes, then turned on her heel and left the kitchen. Trent followed her into the guest bedroom, then pointed to the closet and stood back.

Confused and wondering what might pop out at her, Carrie opened the closet door gingerly.

"Holy crap!"

Trent chuckled. "Interesting reaction. Not exactly what I was hoping for."

Every inch of her spacious closet was taken up with clothes, shoes, purses and unmentionables. Her size, and perfect color choices. She reached out, fingering a finely tailored gray Chanel suit. "Is this the entire women's section of Barneys?"

"Not the entire section, no," he said with absolute seriousness.

She turned and eyeballed him. "Okay, you knew about this job before I even—"

"They left a message here a few hours ago," he confessed without an ounce of remorse.

"You did this in a few hours?"

"It was nothing."

Carrie sat down on her bed and exhaled. She just couldn't fathom how something like this was accomplished in such a short time. But to Trent it really did look effortless. Maybe some calls and a good deal of money was all it took.

Even so, she mused, the gesture was… She looked up at him. "Trent this is great, lovely, thoughtful—"

He stopped her. "Before you say anything further, you should know that this was a purely selfish move on my part."

"Really?"

"With my new position, we have functions to attend, and well, your—"

Her mouth twitched with humor. "My clothes don't cut the mustard. Yes, I'm aware."

"Besides, you do need clothes for work."

She stood up, walked over to him and gave him a hug. With zero hesitation, as though it were meant to be that way, Trent put his arms around her and pulled her in close. His muscles, his scent, the way her breasts always met with his ribs when they were like this—it was all becoming familiar to her.

Her gaze settled on him. "I'm not one of those girls who will act coy and refuse a lovely gift when she really wants to keep it."

"No?"

She shook her head. "I love clothes, dude."

"Did you just call me dude?"

She broke away from him, laughed. "Thank you."

"You're welcome. And now I'm going to finish making dinner before you drink too much wine and get light-headed and attack me."

"I never get light-headed," she called after him.

He frowned at her before leaving the room, muttering to himself like a cranky teenager, "Well, a guy can dream, can't he?"

"Mr. Tanford, there's a Mrs. Davis on the phone for you."

Trent didn't even look up from his work. He didn't recognize the name, and he had a meeting in ten minutes.

"Take a message."

His assistant didn't leave. He heard her clear her throat. "She says it's very important, sir."

"It's always important," Trent uttered. "Take a message."

"She says it's about your mother-in-law."

"I don't have—" He stopped midsentence and processed what his assistant had just said. Yes, he did indeed have a mother-in-law now. He grabbed the phone, "Put her through."

"Yes, sir."

"This is Trent Tanford," he said, curious as to what Carrie's mother might be calling him about. Carrie had mentioned very little about her—just that she lived in town and was an artist, the same information that Trent had gleaned through the investigator.

"Mr. Tanford," came a crackly older voice. "This is Wanda Davis, I'm Mrs. Gray's caretaker."

"Caretaker?" Caretaker for what?

"We have a situation here."

"What kind of situation?"

The woman hesitated. "Do you know where Carrie is, Mr. Tanford?"

"At work." A shot of alarm went through him. He wasn't sure why. "What's this about?"

"I tried to reach her on her cell phone, and at the home number, but it just goes to voice mail. Mrs. Gray is in such a state. Carrie is usually able to calm Mrs. Gray's agitation so we don't have to resort to the trauma of calling an ambulance."

"What? Mrs. Gray is sick?"

"Well, you know, she has…" Wanda paused. "Oh, my. I thought you would know…."

For one brief second Trent thought about his day, his new position and the back-to-back meetings he had scheduled after lunch.

Then he told Wanda in a calm voice, "Don't call an ambulance. I'll be right there." He grabbed a pen. "I just need the address."

Seven

When Carrie arrived at her mother's apartment, she was close to having a heart attack. She'd been in a meeting with the partners and a new client, and everyone had been asked to turn off their cell phones.

She was never doing that again. Vibrate was going to have to suffice.

She'd listened to the five messages from an increasingly worried Wanda as she'd walked back to her office. Immediately she'd grabbed her purse and left for an early lunch, making sure the assistants knew it was an emergency situation.

The first thing Carrie saw when she walked into the apartment was her mother's frazzled caretaker, pacing in the sunless, shadow-filled kitchen, stopping every few moments to cross herself.

Carrie went to her. "Wanda? What happened?"

Sudden relief flickered across Wanda's pale features when she saw Carrie. The older woman rushed to her, shook her head. "I don't know. She was talking about your father."

"Oh God," Carrie uttered, grief circling her heart.

"She's done that before and...nothing happened. So, this time, I thought she was fine. I was going to make her some soup, then, a moment later she became very agitated, crying, saying she had to find your father, make him listen, bring him back for you."

"No."

"She tried to get up and leave the apartment! She tried to get out the door, Carrie."

"Oh God," Carrie whispered, her stomach clenching in knots. Her mother hadn't tried getting out of the house for six months now.

"I've never seen her so upset. I didn't know what to do. So I called your husband."

Carrie's stomach dipped. "Oh." Trent had no idea about her mother's illness. She hadn't wanted to go there with him until she felt she could trust him with something so personal, not to mention something so scary and painful.

"He's been in there with her for the past thirty minutes," Wanda explained.

"What?" *He was here?*

Carrie's mind went blank. She couldn't imagine the two of them together.

"The moment he got here, he calmed her right down." Carrie barely heard Wanda as she rushed down the hall. "I don't know how he did it."

The door was slightly ajar, and when Carrie entered she found her mother asleep on the bed, looking like a young girl, her pale face relaxed. Trent sat on a chair beside her, a book in his hands. He turned when he heard Carrie come in, put his finger to his lips.

"She just fell asleep," he whispered.

Carrie went to him, put her hands on his shoulders and looked down at her mother's calm, sweet face. "Is she okay?"

"Yeah." He kept his voice low. "She was determined to get out of the house, find your dad."

Tears welled in Carrie's eyes and she shook her head, wishing she could make her mother understand that her father had left a long time ago, and that they were so much better off without him now. But Rachel was falling back into the past more and more these days. Those tangled, painful emotions that were just a whisper of a memory to Carrie were real and vivid in her mother's head.

"How did you get her to calm down?"

"I told her I'd find him for her, and for you."

"No…Trent…"

"I had to, Carrie."

Carrie just nodded, understanding completely.

"She asked me who I was," Trent said, looking up at her. "I told her I was your husband."

"What did she say?"

"At first she wasn't sure who you were, but before she fell asleep she looked at me and pointed at my face and said, 'You're Carrie's husband.'"

Carrie squeezed his shoulders. She couldn't believe he was here, doing this for her. "What book do you have there?"

"Pride and Prejudice."

"A romance?"

"Your mother said it was one of her favorites, so… Anyway, it calmed her down." He shrugged. "And for a romance, it wasn't half-bad."

"Good to know that a literary genius like Jane Austen meets with your approval," Carrie whispered drily.

He cocked his head to one side, studied her.

"What?"

"You remind me of Elizabeth Bennet. She's a smart-ass, too."

Carrie laughed softly. "Yes, she is." Then she took a breath and said, "Listen, why don't you go back to work. I'll take over here."

He shook his head. "No."

"What do you mean no?"

"It's your first week at the company…"

"They'll have to understand."

"They won't. What they will do is fire you."

Carrie stilled. She knew Trent was right. But she

couldn't leave her mother alone. If something happened again, set her mother off again, Wanda would need the extra support.

Trent looked at her with such a serious gaze, she almost stepped back. "I'm staying."

Carrie shook her head. "You can't."

"Why not?"

"You have a job, too."

He gave her an arrogant smile. "I'm the head of a company. I can do anything I want. I've missed three days of work in my entire career. Today I'm spending the fourth with your mother."

"Trent—"

"I'll see you later."

She didn't move. Her mind raced with more questions for this man who was acting like...well, like a husband.

"If she gets worse..." she began.

He assured her, "I'll call you."

This job was her future, her mother's security. She gave his shoulder one last squeeze before releasing him. It was a cold feeling. "I'll be back at five-thirty to take over."

"Sure. Go. Go." He waved her away and went back to his book. "I want to see what this Mr. Darcy character is going to do next."

Carrie smiled at his back, gave one last look to her mother and left the room.

Trent was in bed, reading over a few résumés for the position of senior advertising sales exec when he heard the front door open. It was just after eleven, and he'd been home for several hours after leaving Carrie with her mother around dinnertime. He'd offered to stay with her, but she'd insisted that he go home.

He heard her go into her room, heard her close the door, and after a few minutes believed her to be in bed for the night. Why wouldn't she be? She'd had a long, difficult day.

He went back to his résumés, attempting to defeat his disappointment. But then his door opened and she walked in. His mouth dropped an inch. She was wearing nothing but a silk chemise, one of the creamy white ones he'd ordered for her from La Perla.

As she walked toward him, stood at the foot of his bed, he stared at her in awe. Her face was rosy and scrubbed free of all makeup. Her long dark hair was loose, falling over her shoulders in soft waves, and her full, heavy breasts were barely hidden behind the thin, embroidered silk bodice.

He inhaled, his nostrils flaring.

"Trent," she said softly.

"Stop!"

Startled by the anger and heat in his voice, she froze. "What? What's wrong?"

"Don't come in here dressed like that."

"Why?"

"You know why, Carrie."

Her mouth curved into an understanding smile and

she brazenly lifted the hem of her chemise an inch or two, exposing the white silk panties underneath.

"I'm serious, Carrie," he practically growled, his skin raging with need, his erection clearly visible under the thin sheet that covered him from the waist down. "Now, I'm going to give you five seconds to turn around and leave the room. If you don't, expect to feel my hands on your body and my sheets against your back."

Her green eyes glittered with awareness.

She didn't move.

"One," he began, sitting up, "two…"

She didn't move, but he saw a flicker of a smile on her face.

"Three…"

She took a step toward him.

"…four…"

He didn't say five. What was the point? He was off the bed and had her in his arms in a matter of seconds.

His mouth crushed hers as he pulled her back on the bed. For one brief moment, she was on top of him, looking down into his eyes, and something passed between them that hit Trent deep in his gut. This woman was his. For as long as he wanted her.

Then she pressed her hips into his erection and his mind abandoned him. All he wanted was to taste her, suckle her, crawl inside of her and never come out until they were both breathless and ready for sleep. He flipped her onto her back and devoured her with kisses, starting at the base of her neck.

Carrie released a soft moan and let her head drift to the side, giving him better access. He suckled at the thin cord of muscle that housed her rapid pulse and the blood that flowed through her, giving her life. She moved beneath him, her hips pumping up and down, meeting him, telling him she was ready whenever he was, had been for weeks now.

But Trent was determined to go slow. He was going to claim every inch of her as his own.

Carrie felt a shivering madness in her mind and skin, as if she was on the verge of climax, but was afraid her body wouldn't be able to contain the intensity of what was ahead.

A totally naked Trent had her earlobe between his teeth, nibbling, then suckling and she raked her hands over his shoulders, up until her fingers threaded his hair. "Kiss me, please…" she uttered, coaxing him away from her ear over to her mouth.

"Carrie," he whispered before he captured her mouth with his, his hands slipping behind her back, down until he cupped her buttocks, rocked her against his erection.

She reacted quickly, wrapping her legs around his waist, her hands going to his face in the most intimate, loving of touches. Sex hadn't been a part of her reality for a good two years now, and even then it had been pretty ordinary—nothing at all like this—nothing like Trent and how he touched her, moved her, made her mind whisper with thoughts and dreams she'd never known she'd wanted. But she wanted them now, and she wanted them all with him. And best of all, she knew he'd go there with her. He was so desperate for her and it showed in every kiss, every ragged breath he took.

She was so lucky.

He left her mouth then, blazed kisses down her neck and over her collarbone until he stopped at the thin, silk bodice. With gentle, yet anxious fingers, Trent pulled the straps of her chemise down over her arms, elbows and hands, and as he did, the top of her chemise followed suit, peeling away from her skin, down, down over her belly until it rested on her hips.

Trent's gaze burned with heat as he took in her naked chest, the two heavy globes that begged for his touch, his kiss. Carrie let her head drop back against his pillow, let her nostrils fill with the scent of him as he, too, dropped his head and took one hard nipple into his mouth.

Her breasts had always been sensitive, even wearing a sweater without a bra had at times made her feel restless below the waist. But that little ache was nothing compared to what was happening to her now. As Trent suckled one aching nipple, he used his thumb and forefinger to tease the other, flicking, rolling the hot bud between his fingers until Carrie thought she'd lose her mind.

She pumped her hips, writhed in the tangled sheets, her fingers digging into Trent's scalp. She felt a drop of Trent's seed on her inner thigh, and she lost it. She came quick and hard, crying out like a wounded, desperate animal as her hips thrust as though he was inside her.

"Carrie," Trent whispered, nuzzling her breast as his hand moved between her legs. "Oh, sweetheart. Carrie, you're so wet. Tell me what you need."

As Carrie's orgasm eased, her desire for Trent intensified. "You. Inside me. So deep. My legs…so wide, you—"

Trent was reaching for the drawer in his bedside table before she could say anything more. He ripped open the condom and quickly sheathed himself. After peeling off her chemise and tossing it on the floor, he hovered above her. He opened her legs with his thigh, the hair on his legs tickling her skin, making her body weak, wet and hot with desire.

His erection was poised at the entrance to her body, and Carrie lifted her hips, took him inside her just an inch, just to feel the thickness of him invading her.

They were going to fit perfectly.

Doing this changed everything. She knew it. But her need was too great to examine the irrevocable consequences.

Trent's nostrils flared as he breathed, as he stared down at her like a bull ready to charge.

With a boldness she'd always known she possessed, Carrie put her hands to her breasts, teased her nipples into hard peaks as Trent watched in the light of the bedside lamp.

"You," was all he said before he entered her. One straight, hard thrust into her body.

Carrie cried out, spread her legs wider, wrapped her arms around him and filled her hands with his muscled buttocks. She pressed him deeper inside of her, deeper, until he was against her womb. Then he began to move, every stroke hitting the spot that made her throat tighten, made her breasts tingle, made her desperate and aching and ready to explode.

She wrapped her legs around him and followed his rhythm, pumping with him. Desperate to feel him, not only in her body and on top of her, but in her hands, as well, she slid one hand between them and captured the twin weights at the base of his erection.

He groaned at her actions, and as she played him gently, cupped him, she felt him thicken inside of her, felt his whole body shudder. And then he was moving, quickly, his strokes turning into desperate thrusts, hard, frenzied thrusts that had her gripping the bedsheets for support.

His hands found her breasts and he cupped them as he pumped into her, bucking like an animal, harder and harder until they were both completely out of control.

Then Carrie cried out, climax gripping her, claiming her. Unable to stop himself, Trent followed with one desperate thrust deep into her body before collapsing on top of her, shuddering against her wet, hot skin.

Several minutes passed before either one of them could speak. They lay on their sides, under the sheet,

Trent holding Carrie close against him, her back to his belly, her buttocks against his sated groin.

Carrie felt so calm, more relaxed and peaceful than she had in a long time. Was it the sex, she wondered, or was it lying in her husband's arms? Or was it both, wrapped up in a pink cloud of happiness?

She turned to face him, desperate to see his eyes, see if she could read his reaction to what had just happened between them.

But his eyes were closed, his face peaceful.

Like any persistent, just-mated woman, she did her best to wake him up in a loving, sweet way. She kissed the lids of his eyes, the tip of his nose, then his mouth. It took only a moment for him to respond.

"What is it, woman?" he growled. "Ready for me again, are you?" He reached around her waist and gently spanked her naked bottom.

She laughed, and he opened his eyes and grinned at her. "Like that, do you? I'll have to remember that."

She touched his face. "I like you."

She realized the moment the words were out of her mouth that she was wrong. She didn't like him at all, not anymore. She was over the moon, she was falling for him.

Trent stared at her, his brows coming together in a frown. "What's wrong? Are you okay?"

She nodded.

"Are you sure?" He gathered her in his arms and held her impossibly close. "You look sad. Is it about today?"

She kissed him for his concern. "No. But since you

brought it up, I wanted to thank you for what you did today. For my mom."

"It was for you."

"Thank you."

He didn't say anything for a moment, but continued to hold her tightly against him. When he finally spoke, his tone was soft, cautious. "Why didn't you tell me, Car?"

"I told you about her."

"You told me she was a busy artist."

Carrie rubbed her lips back and forth against his arm. "I don't know."

"Alzheimer's, Carrie. It's a big deal."

"I know that. Believe me, Trent—"

"I'm not scolding you, honey," he said gently. "I care about you, and if I would've known, I could've helped earlier."

She looked at him, slipped her hand behind his neck and pulled him in for a kiss. She had truly misjudged this man. He may have been a playboy, but in his guts, his bones, he was a devoted friend.

"Hey," he whispered against her mouth.

"Hmm."

"Can I ask you one more thing?"

"Of course."

"What about your father?"

She stiffened in his arms, and she knew he'd felt it. But he didn't let go. "What about him?"

"Why didn't you tell me he walked out on you?"

So, her mother had experienced a few lucid moments when Trent was there last night.

She tried to disentangle herself from his grasp. But he wouldn't allow it. He held her firmly. She stopped fighting and said quickly, "Same reason I didn't tell you about my mother. It was all too personal."

"Too personal?"

"Our marriage was supposed to be a business arrangement, Trent. It wasn't supposed to get personal, or sexual, for that matter."

"But it has." He released her then, and she sat up. "I want it to stay that way, Carrie." She turned to stare at him, not sure she'd heard him correctly. He nodded. "You need to tell me everything."

Her gaze flickered. "I don't know if I can agree to that, Trent."

"Why not?"

"One year. That's all we promised each other." She felt a strong need to protect herself at that moment. "We're not like a real married couple, sharing pasts and hopes for the future. This is amazing, you are amazing, but it hasn't been long enough…. No matter how I feel about you—"

"And how is that?"

She shook her head. She couldn't. There was no way she was going to tell this man that she was falling in love with him. Not until he said it first. If he ever said it.

She started again. "No matter how I feel about you, I honestly don't know if I can trust you."

"Carrie—"

The cell phone beside the bed rang. Carrie and Trent stared at each other as it continued. Then Carrie gestured to the BlackBerry and said, "Go ahead."

Trent reached for the phone.

Carrie pulled the covers over her body as she listened to him answer, then say, "Yes. What? Okay, fine."

He slipped off the bed. "I have to go."

"It's close to midnight," Carrie said, feeling cold suddenly.

"I know."

"Everything okay?"

He grabbed clothes from his closet and dressed quickly. "Yes. Nothing to worry about."

Carrie watched him. "Don't exactly trust me, either, do you?"

His jaw was tight as he walked back to the bed. He leaned down and kissed her on the mouth. "Be here when I get back?"

She sighed. They had a long way to go. She and her husband. They both wanted the one thing the other didn't seem willing to give—trust. But after tonight, as she'd predicted earlier when Trent's arms were around her and his shaft was buried inside of her, nothing was ever going to be the same. Everything would change. It had to.

But perhaps trusting each other would be a part of that change.

Her past, her father.

Trent's present, where he was running off to in the middle of the night.

She nodded, said, "I'll be here," and he left the room.

Eight

"There better be a damn good reason why you've asked me to come down here."

In a drab, worn office, across a cluttered desk, Detective McGray took the toothpick out of his mouth and addressed Trent and the new lawyer who sat behind him. "I'm not here to waste your time, Mr. Tanford, or to take you away from that pretty new wife of yours."

Trent's jaw tightened with annoyance. "What is it you want, then?"

"I wanted to show you this."

The detective slid a piece of paper across his desk. And both Trent and his new lawyer, Jerry Devlin, leaned forward and took a look.

"The threatening letter you received," McGray began, "did it look something like this?"

Trent scanned the page.

One million.
Grand Cayman island account.
One week to comply.

The next part, however, was blocked out with black tape, presumably by the police, so Trent couldn't see what the letter writer had threatened the receiver with.

He looked up. "Yes. Looks exactly the same."

McGray nodded. "Okay. Good. Thank you. That's all."

"That's all?"

"We needed to know if the letter matched this one, the first one."

Trent lost it. "Why didn't you have me look at this the last time I was here? In the middle of the damned day?"

"At that time we didn't think it was appropriate."

"But midnight on a weeknight is?"

Devlin put a hand on Trent's shoulder. "Mr. Tanford, please."

"Yes, easy, Mr. Tanford. An agitated witness in a police station can be…" Detective McGray stopped talking as he caught sight of something in the window behind Trent and stood up. "Excuse me a minute."

"Sure, why not," Trent muttered darkly as the man walked out. "This is ridiculous."

"True," Devlin admitted, "but it seems to be over

and done. Let's just keep things relaxed. We don't want the word on the street to be that the head of AMS won't cooperate with the police."

"Fine," Trent ground out.

The lawyer frowned. "I'm going to have a talk with the detective, see if we can move things along, all right?"

"Good idea."

A few minutes later, a man in his midfifties with a stocky frame and a full head of dark hair stuck his very familiar face into the detective's office.

"Trent? Hey, how are you?"

The police captain, who was a longtime friend of the Tanford family, offered his hand.

Trent stood and shook the man's hand. "Good, Mike. A little tired, though."

"Yeah, sorry about that. I'm afraid it had to be done."

"If you say so."

"Case isn't moving forward, and we're getting a lot of pressure from the city." He leaned in. "Between you and me?"

Trent nodded.

Mike's voice dropped to a whisper. "We believe Marie Endicott's death may not be a suicide after all."

Trent frowned. "What? Why not?"

The man's brows lifted. "That I can't tell you. But I appreciate you coming in tonight. Say hello to your mother and father for me."

"Sure."

"And congratulations on your marriage. Never

thought I'd see the day." He winked. "She must be something else."

"She is." Trent had never been the kind of man who talked trash or shared anything personal about the women he was seeing, and he wasn't about to start now.

The two men shook hands and the captain left the room, just as the detective and Trent's attorney returned.

McGray didn't sit down. Instead he gestured for Trent and the lawyer to follow him. They walked out of his office, down the hall and to the door of the precinct. "Thanks for coming in. I'll let you know if I need you or Mrs. Tanford for anything else."

Trent bristled. What the hell was the detective doing? Offering up a threat? Making sure Trent stayed in line and jumped to attention anytime the man called?

"You need to leave my wife out of this," Trent said.

Devlin jumped in quickly. "What Mr. Tanford is trying to say—"

"No, Jerry," Trent interrupted caustically. "What I'm saying to the detective is very simple. My wife has nothing to do with any of this."

McGray's face was a mask of composure. "I'm sure you're right, but you never know."

"I know," Trent insisted, his tone as sharp as a blade. "And I don't want her dragged through a worthless question-and-answer session."

With a shrug, McGray said casually, "If I don't have to, I promise I won't. But I'll expect you to bring forward anything new that comes your way."

Two minutes later, Trent walked out of the police station, stepped into his waiting town car and slammed the door. He couldn't believe he'd actually left his wife curled up in his sheets, naked and warm for thirty-five minutes of total BS.

But as the car sped away, as he leaned back against the leather seat and released a weighty breath or two, he realized that for the first time in his life he actually had someone to go home to. That reality had the power to change his humor into something altogether new to him, something resembling contentment.

When Trent crawled into his warm bed twenty minutes later, he caught the scent of lovemaking in his nostrils and inhaled deeply. It was everywhere, that addictive scent: on the sheets, pillows, and on Carrie's soft, sleeping frame.

He tried to will his erection away as he pulled her to him, but it was impossible, especially when she arched her back and moved her buttocks against him.

"Hey," she whispered.

"Hey." He kissed the back of her neck, suddenly relieved to be home, in his bed, holding her.

"Everything okay?" she asked.

"Fine."

"Do you want to tell me about it?"

"Not tonight."

"Okay. But you're—"

"I'm fine. I promise."

"Okay."

Again, she pressed back against his erection, and his hands went around her waist to her stomach, then moved upward until he cupped her breasts. Her breathing changed as he rolled her nipples between his fingers, and against his pulsing shaft he felt the warm heat of her body.

Ready and willing.

They made love into the early-morning hours, welcoming the crimson dawn with cries of pleasure and need and release.

"I have something to tell you and I don't want you to freak out."

A few days later, Carrie sat on a plump pedicure spa chair, her feet dangling in a hot, soapy whirlpool tub, her two friends bracketing her. Since Amanda had been in New York working diligently on next month's party for 721 Park Avenue's historical landmark status, the tall blonde knew exactly what Carrie was about to say. Julia, on the other hand, had been in Bermuda with her new husband and had no clue as to the goings-on in Carrie's life over the past couple of weeks.

The pregnant blonde eyed Carrie curiously. "Does this have something to do with why you never e-mailed me back during my trip?"

"Sort of."

"By the way, Jules, I can't believe you took the time to e-mail anyone," Amanda quipped, holding up two bottles of nail polish, trying to decide which shade of pink would work best with her skin tone. "You were on your honeymoon, for God's sake."

"So?"

Amanda looked nonplussed. "You should have been doing honeymoon-type things."

Patting her round stomach, Jules said, "The belly's starting to get in the way, okay?"

"Really?"

"Really."

"Can't you just try it from be—"

"Oh my lord, Amanda!" Julia cried, feigning shock and horror at her friend's dirty little mind.

Carrie couldn't stand it anymore. She inhaled deeply, then blurted out her secret. "I married Trent Tanford."

Both women forgot what they had been talking about and turned to stare at her. Amanda just grinned and shook her head, while Jules looked at Carrie as if she'd just grown a second head.

"Excuse me? What?"

"I married Trent. Tanford. My neighbor."

"Oh, I know who he is, Carrie." Julia stared at her for a good minute, perhaps trying to read on her forehead the answer of why Carrie had done what she'd done. Finally she said, "Why?"

Carrie's gaze dropped. "I fell in love with him."

But Jules wasn't about to let it go at that. "When did you fall in love with him?"

Carrie exhaled. She'd expected this, especially from Julia, but she knew it was only because the woman cared about her. The problem was that Carrie didn't want to share the details of her marriage and how it came about with anyone. Firstly, because the reasons were embarrassing. And secondly, because she would have to admit that she didn't marry a man for love—and that was a painful thing to admit.

No one needed to know how her marriage had begun, only how it was now.

"Listen," she said to Jules, "I know this is crazy and sudden and crazy again, but it is what it is. I love the guy."

Now. She loved him now. And that was all that mattered.

A sweet, gentle feeling moved through Carrie at the admission. Yes, she really did love him.

She looked from Julia to Amanda and back to Julia again. "Now, I was hoping for warm wishes and heart-felt congratulations." Carrie held up a hand. "Not because we're friends, mind you, but because I'm treating the two of you to this mani-pedi."

Julia looked as though she wanted to continue with the questions, but instead she smiled, sighed and leaned back in her chair. "And you think you can just bribe your way out of a friendly interrogation with a sugar-and-chocolate foot massage?"

"That was the hope, yes."

Beside Carrie, Amanda let out a sigh of ecstasy. "I think I can forgive you, Car."

Julia snorted. "Traitor."

The three sat in silence for a few minutes, enjoying the hot, swirling water, but soon a woman's need to discuss, chat and interrogate once again became overwhelming.

"So, how *is* married life?" Julia asked.

"You would know, Jules," Amanda pointed out.

"I wouldn't know how it is to be married to Trent."

Carrie smiled. "Surprising, actually."

Julia lifted her perfectly manicured brows. "Interesting choice of verbiage."

"Surprising how?" Amanda asked, handing her choice of polish to the technician with a gracious smile. "Little notes under your pillow when you wake up surprising? Or a closet full of whips and chains kind of surprising?"

Julia laughed as Carrie answered, "The first. He's amazing, really thoughtful and caring. He treats me like a queen. It's not at all what I had expected." Especially after the deal he'd offered way back when—that straight-up business deal that he'd offered. That one she'd agreed to.

For a moment, Carrie wondered what Trent thought of her and their marriage now. Did he care for her as much as she cared for him? Was he sitting in a sports bar, talking to his friends about her?

She guessed, probably not.

"Well, you knew some of that, right?" Jules asked. "Before you married him? I mean, that's what made you marry him so quickly, right? Finding out he was this amazing guy and falling in love with that guy?"

"Right," Carrie said quickly. "Of course. I'm just

saying that even though I saw his sweet side before I married him, he was such a player when we met that I was worried, a bit, that maybe he'd never come to heel, so to speak." Carrie stopped herself before her ramblings sounded any more incoherent.

"I get it," Julia said, acting as though she did indeed understand.

Amanda looked at Carrie, worry behind her steely gray eyes. "Just be careful, Carrie."

"Why?"

"Don't make the mistake of thinking you can change a man."

"I don't," Carrie assured her. "I'm not."

"I'm not trying to be a downer, I swear, it's just in my experience…"

"What experience is that?" Carrie asked, suddenly curious. Despite being such an outgoing personality, Amanda had never been all that open about her past.

But Amanda didn't share anything of worth. She shrugged, her gaze on the tub of swirling water before her, her lovely face blank all of a sudden, as though she were trying to hide her emotions from the two of them.

Without missing a beat, Julia stepped in and returned to her favorite topic of the day. Although this time she brought along a brand-new perspective. "Maybe Trent was a player who was waiting for the real thing to come along."

Carrie liked that assessment, and grinned. "I think so." *I hope so.*

Julia held up a hand. "By the way, I want it on the record that it was my idea to have Carrie knock on his door and rip him a new one, which has clearly led to her happiness and a lifelong love."

Amanda looked up, shook her head. "We both encouraged her."

"I don't remember it that way."

"Stop right there, ladies." Grinning at her friends, Carrie attempted to make peace. "Since it is my happiness you are both trying to take credit for, I will just say thank you to you, Julia, and you, Amanda—because honestly, without that little push, I wouldn't be where I am today…very happy and in love."

"You're welcome, Car," Amanda said quickly.

"Yes, congrats, girl." And with that, Julia leaned back in her chair and sighed as the technician began massaging her feet.

Carrie eyed her hopefully. "So, you do forgive me for not e-mailing you back, right, Jules?"

The woman was so lost to the sweet scent of rose oil and the killer hands of Jeanne Marie that she barely registered the question. Her eyes closed, she muttered a clipped, "Huh? Oh, yeah, sure. Whatever."

Carrie turned and looked at Amanda. The two women laughed at their friend, then leaned back in their chairs, closed their eyes and followed her lead.

Nine

Schmoozing with important clients was standard fare in Trent's business. Normally, he did it solo, and had never felt as though a client's respect for him diminished because of his singleton status. But tonight, he saw his world through very different eyes—married eyes—and he was a little shocked to realize that his father may have been right in his belief that persons in high levels of business gain more respect when a wedding ring is attached to their finger and a wife is attached to their side.

Now, his wife had left his side about an hour ago, but only to work the room—something Trent had neither asked her to do, nor even thought about her doing when they'd stepped out of the black limousine and into Nanni on East Forty-sixth.

AMS had rented out the entire restaurant for this event. Hosting the brass from the top AMS affiliate stations on the West Coast was a big deal, particularly for Trent, as this was his first major event as head of the network. His father was out of the country, so Trent and Carrie were the only Tanfords in attendance.

Trent watched Carrie tuck into the center of a group of females—some execs, some wives—with the grace and ease of a practiced socialite. She looked amazing in a pale pink strapless dress that hugged her breasts and fell in a gentle wave down the rest of her body. Her hair was back in a simple, chic bun at the nape of her neck and her makeup was natural and young—just like her.

A waiter silently offered him a risotto puff, which he declined.

He had realized only a few days ago that he was completely over the edge for Carrie. Understanding this fact had put his past relationship into perspective, ending his moratorium on marriage for good. His fiancée had been a young man's crush, unsustainable lust masquerading as something far stronger.

He knew this because he felt that "something stronger" for his wife.

Every time he looked at her he wanted to wrap his hands around her and take her away with him. Every time another man looked at her, he wanted to put his fist through a wall. And there had been several of those

West Coast playboy bachelor types asking if she was taken, and by whom.

She made him feel like a freaking caveman.

"I've never felt envy, Tanford."

Trent looked at the man who had just given him a thumping pat on the back, then followed his line of vision. Alan Dowd was the President and General Manager of one of AMS's largest affiliates in Los Angeles, and was also a longtime friend of Trent's father.

Alan had his gaze trained on Carrie, as she conversed easily with a group of affiliates from Oregon and Washington State. "No. Never felt envious of a man until tonight, that is."

Trent nodded, said pleasantly, professionally, "I am a lucky man."

"Damn right. Don't let that one get away."

"Not possible, Alan. She married me."

The man raised his brows. "Never a guarantee. My ex-wife is living with her new lover in our house in Tahiti and I go to sleep with a folder full of absurd complaints from the Human Resources Department."

While the easy response to a comment like that would've been to laugh, joke around and commiserate, Trent was a seasoned pro. To act like just another "guy" would've deemed him totally unprofessional when Alan reflected on the matter later on. And when Alan was back in his hotel room sobering up, he would've reflected.

So, Trent didn't take the conversation further, but he

did smile broadly, tell the man it was good to see him and that continued success in Los Angeles was expected, and then he walked away, moved on to the GM of his Utah affiliate.

As the night was drawing to a close, Trent made his way over to Carrie, who smiled with her mouth and with her eyes as if she were very glad to see him.

He put his arm around her waist and whispered in her ear, "Ready?"

"Absolutely."

They said their goodbyes to a few remaining guests before heading out of the restaurant and onto East Forty-sixth. They waited only a moment for the limousine to navigate through the heavy midtown traffic and pull up to the restaurant. Trent waved at the driver to remain in the car and he opened the door for Carrie.

When he slid in beside her and shut the door, she dropped back against the seat and exhaled. "Okay, I hate to say this, Trent, because I know you do business with these people, but tonight was—"

"Tedious?"

She grimaced. "I told you I hated to say it."

"My work can be that way at times."

"No, it's not your work."

He grinned. "All right, the people can be tedious at times."

"Actually most of the people were fine. It was just a few of the executives."

"Daniel Embry?"

She pointed at him. "Yes. He was killer dull. Fly fishing and marble collecting…"

"How about Megan Frost?"

"Well, she was just plain nuts."

"And that boyfriend of hers—"

"No," Carrie interrupted, "I think he was an escort. The hired type. And an actor. The guy wouldn't stop talking about himself and asking anyone around him if they knew Andrew Lloyd Webber." She rolled her eyes. "I just wanted to say, 'Step out of the eighties, buddy!'"

Trent laughed and said, "Yeah, but his tattoo was cool."

Carrie laughed with him, and the pretty sound reverberated off the walls of the car and through Trent's chest. He pulled her to him and gave her a kiss. He couldn't help himself. "You were amazing tonight."

She cuddled in close to him. "Thank you."

"A natural."

She shrugged in his arms. "Just doing my duty."

His mouth twitched with amusement. "Well, then it's my duty to give you a proper thank-you."

She grinned. "Oh, my."

Trent's gaze never left hers as he called, "Excuse me?"

The chauffeur answered quickly. "Yes, sir?"

"Circle the park, say…three times before you take us home."

"Yes, sir."

"Three times?" Carrie repeated, her brows drifting up. "What are you planning, Tanford?"

Trent depressed a black button to his right and the

privacy partition went up. Every window was tinted and soundproof, but Trent switched on some music just to be safe.

The smooth and sexy sounds of Ne-Yo moved through the speakers as Trent left Carrie's side and planted himself at her feet.

"What are you doing?" she asked him, her green eyes glittering with playful intent.

He took off her shoes, one at a time. "You spent quite a few hours on your feet tonight. They must be sore." His gaze remained on hers as he massaged her feet.

She sighed, relaxed back against the black leather seat. Trent watched her hungrily. Married life surprised the hell out of him. He was happy, satisfied and completely unconcerned that his four-week rule was fast approaching. Carrie was different. She was his, his wife, his heart.

Carrie had cured him of all of it.

When her feet relaxed against his palms, he moved on to her ankles, her calves. He felt his body go rigid, his breath quicken as his hands lifted her skirt. Carrie opened her eyes, watched him as he eased the pink silk all the way up to her hips.

Her chest lifted and lowered in quick succession as her breathing changed. She watched his hands move to her inner thigh, upward, then disappear beneath the short hem of her dress as he found the warm, wet center of her.

She moaned and arched her back.

Trent thought he was going to climax right then and

there, but he bit his lip and curled his fingers around the pale pink strip of lace that covered the sweet heaven he wanted so badly to taste.

In seconds, her panties were down her thighs, around her ankles and in Trent's suit coat pocket.

Trent could barely breathe. He was really badly off. Hell-bent on giving her pleasure, tasting her, having her scent mark him, having her scent on him all night long.

He reached out, gently splayed her legs, then ran his finger down the center of her, so softly and slowly she lifted her hips to follow his hand as it moved.

He groaned at her reaction.

"What's wrong?" she whispered.

"Nothing. You're so wet."

Her eyes were glassy with desire as she smiled at him. "It's you. The way you touch me."

Her honesty, the way she stared at him, as though she totally trusted him with her body, did something to him and he spoke recklessly, like a tyrant, but he didn't care. "You're mine, Carrie. No one touches you but me. Ever. Do you understand?"

Carrie heard his words, but she could hardly register them. Trent had placed himself between her thighs, and his fingers were pressing the soft folds of her core open. Then his tongue was on her, on the sensitive peak inside, and she moaned and let her head fall back. She was limp and high and wanted to press his head closer.

His tongue lapped at the hard bud deep in her cleft, sending her flying as her hips lifted and lowered. Carrie had no control of her body; it moved and undulated and begged Trent to continue to lick her. He did, and as he did, he slipped one hand underneath her buttocks while his fingers played her, flicking, circling the wet opening to her body.

Then when her breath was coming quick and ragged, he plunged two fingers inside of her.

Carrie cried out, gulped air as white-hot stars imprinted on her closed eyelids.

She was on the edge of climax. Trent must've felt it, too, because he didn't stay still for long. He thrust his fingers in and out of her in quick, hard movements, simulating his sex as his tongue continued to lap at her swollen cleft.

She writhed against him, pumped her hips, dug her nails into the leather seat, and then it hit—climax, wave after wave of rioting spasms inside her.

She lifted her hips, held there. She couldn't breathe, she couldn't think.

And then the fog lifted and her hips lowered and she continued to pump against his mouth, but in slower and slower movements until she finally stilled.

After a moment, Trent took his mouth from her, but kept his fingers inside of her, still thrusting gently as her climax eased.

He watched her face, smiled when she smiled at him, and as they rounded the park for the third time, Carrie managed to find her voice enough to utter the words, "You are so welcome, honey."

* * *

When they pulled up to the apartment and got out, they were both disheveled and acting like two teenagers with hard-ons. They held hands and kissed each other madly as they walked through the thick mahogany doors.

They weren't even close to being finished with each other. That quick, hot detour in the limousine was just the beginning, and Carrie hated to admit it, but she understood now, without even a breath of jealousy, why women showed up at Trent's door at 2:00 a.m.

He was amazing.

And all hers.

The massive lobby was pretty dead except for the presence of Vivian Vannick-Smythe and her two yappy little dogs, who were both dressed to the gaudy nines, as usual.

The crystal chandelier overhead was too bright after the dim coolness of the limo. Carrie wanted to bury her head in Trent's jacket so she wouldn't be noticed and have to chat with the woman or anyone else who crossed their path tonight. She just wanted to get upstairs and be alone with Trent, have him all to herself.

And this time, *she* wanted to touch *him*, feel him in her hands, make him come apart, make his legs shake and his head spin.

Vivian stood beside the wide mahogany desk in the center of lobby, chatting with Henry Brown, the doorman. The mousy young man and the unconventional older woman were deep in conversation and it took the loud, echoing click clack of Carrie's heels against the ivory marble floors to jar them both.

"Hello, Vivian," Trent said smoothly as he and Carrie walked toward the elevator.

Vivian smiled in a panicky sort of way and muttered, "Hello, Trent," then quickly walked away from Henry, although Carrie noticed that her little dogs lingered at his feet.

Frustrated with the odd behavior of her dogs, Mrs. Vannick-Smythe gave a hard yank on their leashes before they gave up on Henry and followed the woman outside.

"What was that all about?" Carrie said as the elevator doors closed.

"Never can tell with that woman."

And that was all he was going to say on the subject, it seemed, because he'd barely touched the button for the twelfth floor before he had Carrie around the waist and pressed back against the elevator wall. His blue eyes flashed with deviousness as his knee moved between her thighs. He leaned in and he found her ear, nibbled the lobe. "I want to smell like you all night."

Ripples of hot anticipation went through Carrie's body and she grinned to herself, her eyes closing. If she had her way, Trent Tanford was never going to say those words to another woman.

His tongue flicked gently against her ear, then a soft puff of air. Her skin went up in flames and melted against him as her arms went around his neck. They made out all the way up to their floor, stumbled down the hall, barely made it into his apartment before his coat and tie were off and her dress was up around her hips.

After Trent fumbled with the key, opened the door, they pushed their way in and settled in the hall, barely hearing the phone ring.

"Don't answer it," she uttered.

He chuckled. "Are you kidding?"

Carrie dropped back against the wall as Trent dived for her, trailing hot kisses down her neck, over her collarbone. He yanked down the top of her dress, freeing her breasts.

That's when Carrie took control. She wanted him, wanted to feel his shaft in her hands, kneel at his feet and take him into her mouth, know that he was watching her suckle him just as she'd watched him with his head between her thighs in the limo.

She grabbed him around the waist and turned them both, so he was the one backed up against the wall. As somewhere in the house the phone continued to ring, Carrie grinned and started to undo Trent's belt, then his zipper. They were both breathing heavy as the machine kicked in.

"Mr. Tanford, Detective McGray here."

Carrie stilled, her fingers deep into the waistband of his boxers.

"You left your BlackBerry at the station the other night. When you come by to get it, could you stop in and see me, I have one more question about that letter, and about your—" the man paused, then "—*time* with Ms. Endicott."

When the phone clicked off, Carrie stepped back, pulled up her dress to cover her breasts. "Who's Detective McGray?"

"No one." Trent went to her, tried to kissed her, tried to get her mind back in the game, back on him, on them.

But Carrie wasn't having any of that. Her skin had grown cold in mere seconds. "Was he talking about Marie Endicott?"

Realizing that their moment of pleasure was over, Trent exhaled and said, "Yes."

Anxiety threatened to suffocate her. "That's where you were the other night? The police station."

"Carrie, you need to calm down."

"Were you called in for questioning about her death?"

"Yes—"

"But it was a suicide," she fairly shouted, panic hitting her full force.

His gaze flickered. "They're not so sure about that anymore."

"What?" She stared at him, her heart hammering painfully in her chest. "Oh my God. Are you a suspect?"

Ten

Trent stood in the hall, where not ten seconds ago he was happily making out with his wife. He didn't like the way Carrie was looking at him, accusatory and ready to believe the worst. But he was cool and calm when he spoke. "Several people in the building were called into the station to talk with police, Carrie."

"I wasn't," she said indignantly.

"Well, you didn't know her."

"And you did."

"Yes."

"You used to date her, didn't you?"

He threw his hands up. "Oh my God." He was so sick of this subject. "It was two dates. It was nothing."

But obviously Carrie didn't think so. "If it was nothing, the police wouldn't be calling here or having you come down to the station in the middle of the night." She cocked her head to the side. "What was that all about? Down at the station, eleven o'clock on a weeknight? Must've been pretty important."

Trent could feel his patience wearing thin. Why didn't he just come clean about the letter, make things easy and simple?

Maybe because nothing was ever simple when it came to women—and this woman in particular. He had a sneaking suspicion that she didn't want to believe him, whatever he said. "They had questions, Carrie. They wanted to know if I knew anything about why she might have taken her life."

"And did you?"

"No," he said emphatically.

She paused, and he thought for one brief shining moment that she was going to drop it. But her gaze searched his, looking for more. "You're not telling me everything, are you?"

He started to walk away. "I'm done here."

"Wait a minute. What about the suicide not being a suicide at all?"

"Good night, Carrie."

"Are you seriously going to walk out on this conversation?"

He whirled on her. "This isn't a conversation. This is an interrogation."

"Well, you should be used to those by now."

Anger bled from his veins. "You are…"

"What?" she urged, her green eyes flashing.

"Unbelievable. You're acting like—"

"Like what?" she interrupted. "Like a wife?"

He stared at her, his nostrils flaring. "I was going to say like a crazy person."

He saw her emotionally take a step back. She looked down, bit her lip. When she looked back up at him, he saw tears in her eyes. Her voice was raspy and tired. "Well, maybe I am crazy. Maybe I'm crazy to have thought that this could be a real marriage, where the two people in it shared stuff with each other."

Trent's gut twisted. "Like how you shared 'stuff' about your father with me? Or your mother's illness?"

His words caught her off guard, and he saw her shut down immediately. "I'm tired," she whispered, walking past him toward her room.

Trent stood there, shaking his head. "Yeah, so am I."

Carrie sat on the edge of her bed, feeling like a brat, like an ass, like a freaking two-year-old who wouldn't share her toys, but expected every other kid in the play-group to share theirs.

What the hell had just happened back there? Never in her life had she reacted that way, treated someone with such disrespect and zero tolerance.

Trent was right, she was completely nuts.

And obviously desperately in love.

Why else would she react that way? Lashing out at the man completely out of fear…

Outside her window, the lights of the city flickered under the dark sky. She had asked for the truth from him, but if she looked at herself honestly, she hadn't wanted to hear the truth at all. What she'd wanted to do was jump to the part when he confessed to something so foul she had no choice but to leave him.

She exhaled, put her head in her hands. Was that what she was doing? Using her daddy abandonment issues on him? Finding an excuse to leave him before he left her?

Outside her door, she heard the television click on, and some type of sports game blared through the surround sound speakers.

She had to right this. She had to talk to him. If she didn't, they didn't have a chance of moving beyond tonight, much less making it a year.

She grabbed her hairbrush from her purse and a pair of white underwear from her drawer and left the room.

As expected, Trent was in the living room, sprawled out on the couch, his gaze plastered to the TV. Baseball. The Yankees were playing someone, but Carrie gave the game little notice.

Her heart knocked around in her chest as she stood behind the couch. She dropped the panties over her brush, then reached over his head and waved the white underwear in front of his face.

He stilled, then looked over his shoulder at her and

said evenly, "Is that supposed to be a come-on or your perverse way of offering a truce?"

She pulled the brush back and shrugged. "Whatever gets us back into the elevator." She gave him a half smile and added, "Metaphorically speaking."

Amusement flickered in his eyes. "Have a seat."

Carrie walked around the couch. Trent turned off the game, and she sat in front of him on the coffee table.

"How about I go first?" she said.

"Okay."

"I'm sorry."

He took her hand in his and nodded. "I'm sorry, too."

The knot in her stomach eased at his quick acceptance of her apology, not to mention offering his own apology, which really wasn't something he had needed to offer at all. "That was unacceptable behavior—how I reacted to you back there. I've never spoken to anyone that way in my life."

"Wow, I feel honored," he said, humor still flickering in his gaze.

Carrie took a deep breath and tried to find a place to begin. "I was nine when my father left. I wish I could say he gave no warning, but he always warned us. Maybe he was just not into being a dad, or maybe he was just into messing with our minds, I don't know. But it was always, 'One day you won't have me to bring home a paycheck. One day you won't have me to play with or to put you to sleep or to teach you to fish or to…' well, fill in the blank. Then one day, he wasn't around."

She felt Trent squeezing her hand and it gave her the courage to keep going. "And maybe I was relieved. But I think it's made me wary of guys, and unwilling to trust them. Clearly, it has. I just didn't notice it before. There've been no long-term relationships before." She shrugged. "I always ended it before it got too serious, so it *wouldn't* get serious, you know?"

Trent nodded, smiled. "Yes. I do know."

She grinned. "Been protecting yourself, too?"

"Yes, but for a very different reason."

She didn't push him on that. It was her time to come clean. She held his gaze. "I didn't tell you about my father because honestly, I can't let myself completely trust you yet."

Trent said nothing for a moment, just looked at her. Then he lifted her hand to his mouth and kissed her cold fingers. "I understand, and I respect that."

"But I want to trust you."

"I want you to."

"I want to trust you because—" She paused. She paused because she was about to say the most important three words she'd ever said to a man, and she was afraid. But in the spirit of coming clean, she stumbled ahead. "I want to trust you because I love you."

She waited for him to react, look appalled or worse. But he didn't. He didn't look readable at all, and that freaked her out so much that when he did open his mouth to say something, she stopped him. "Please don't. Don't reply to that. I just want to put it out there by itself for now, okay?"

His eyes grew suddenly dark, yet very, very warm. He nodded, squeezed her hand again and said, "All right. We'll leave it."

"Good. Thanks."

But he added a pointed, "For now."

She nodded, breathed a sigh of relief. She just couldn't deal with his rejection right now.

He leaned forward in his seat. "I think it's my turn."

"Okay," she said with a touch of unease.

"Several months ago, I went out on a date with Marie Endicott. She was a nice woman, funny. But we had nothing in common and after the second date we both agreed there wouldn't be a third. I saw her in the building a few times and we said hello. But that was it." His voice faltered slightly on the next part. "Then the news came of her suicide. Horrible news."

He released a breath. "A few weeks ago I received an anonymous letter. Whoever sent it wanted me to wire a million dollars into an account on Grand Cayman Island or else they would expose my past indiscretions—which I later realized was my nonrelationship with Marie. Since I'd only dated her twice and had nothing to hide, I had originally dismissed the letter. I thought it was BS, someone messing with me, and I threw it away."

"Anyway, the cops called me in to question me about my relationship with Marie, see if I knew anything, and while I was there the first time, I mentioned the letter.

They told me of a similar letter that had been sent to someone in the building."

"Who?" Carrie asked, her curiosity piqued.

Trent shook his head. "They wouldn't tell me. But when I was called to come back in just recently, they showed me the letter. They wanted to know if it was the same."

"Was it?"

Trent nodded. "Pretty much, although they'd blocked out the section with the threat, so I couldn't see that part."

Carrie shook her head, thinking of people in the building. "I wonder who it was sent to." She wondered if Julia or Amanda knew anything about Marie or the letter. But she couldn't really come out and ask them, could she? This was Trent's business, and she wasn't about to share something that personal, even with her friends.

"One last thing," Trent said, capturing her attention once again. "When I was there, the captain, who's a friend of my family's, mentioned that they're starting to think that Marie's death might not be a suicide at all. But he wouldn't expound on that."

Carrie released a heavy breath. "Wow."

"Yeah."

"So, that's it?"

"That's it." He lifted her hand again, kissed her fingers again.

With a slow grin on her face, she looked him over. "No skeletons hidden in your pockets?"

He lifted his arms. "Come check my pockets for yourself."

Laughing, she went to him, sat on his lap and put her arms around his neck. "Was this our first fight?"

"Mmm-hmm." He pulled her close. "And because we had to endure such an unpleasant first fight, I think we should be rewarded with superhot first makeup—"

"Sex?" she offered, then laughed.

"Yes." He eased her off his lap, then stood. "But not here."

"What?"

"Hold on a sec." He left the room, and when he came back, he took her hand and led her out of the apartment.

"Where are we going?" she asked as they walked down the hall.

When Trent got to the elevator, he pressed the down button. "You said, 'whatever gets us back to the elevator.'" He bowed his head. "All I want to do is please you, darling."

Awareness shot through Carrie's body, heating her skin. The elevator doors opened, and as Trent ushered her inside, she laughed softly, like a naughty little girl. "But what about the residents? They won't be able to use—"

The doors had hardly closed when Trent captured her mouth.

The elevator had barely moved before Trent reached out and flicked the emergency stop button.

"But, Trent—" Carrie inhaled sharply as he pressed

her back against the elevator wall, pulled down the top of her dress, filled his hands with her breasts.

"We'll be quick," he murmured, lowering his head.

His tongue lapped at her nipple and she gasped, groaned.

"Not too quick." Every inch below her waist was aching, throbbing.

"Just long enough for you to come."

He snaked a warm hand up her dress, his fingers brushing her inner thigh. She gripped the steel railing as he found her, wet and ready for him. "Yeah...that could be pretty quick." He slipped two fingers deep inside of her. Her breath caught in her throat. "Oh, oh, my, oh, Trent, oh, g—"

Ten minutes later, mousy doorman Henry Brown had canceled the emergency call to the elevator repair company, and the building's irritated residents were finally making their way up to their respective apartments.

Carrie and Trent sitting in a tree.

K-I-S-S-I-N-G.

First comes love, then comes marriage. Then comes...

Wait a second!

First came marriage.

Laughing at her girlhood song, Carrie glanced at the clock on her laptop. It was after six. Dammit. She had a date with a very important lady tonight, and if she didn't hustle she was going to miss it.

She straightened her desk, switched off her computer and grabbed her purse. Things were going very well at her new job. She'd managed to impress everyone in her department with her efficiency and ever-present creative ideas.

Most of the staff had already left for the day, though a few workaholics still remained at their desks, glued to their computer monitors. She called out a cheery goodbye to them as she headed for the elevators.

She was so lucky. Hers was truly a dream job, and she had Trent to thank for the opportunity.

Trent. Her husband. Her lover.

She punched the *L* and sailed down toward the lobby, all the while recalling her ten minutes in heaven with him in their own building's elevator the other night.

A shiver of awareness moved through her as the doors opened. But it was quickly defeated by the sharp, oddly shaped, hundred-pound boulder she'd been carrying around in her chest ever since she'd gone completely insane and said those three words to Trent.

Outside, the manic heat of the day had barely subsided, and the delightful scent of urine and sweaty pedestrians assaulted her. She went to the curb and hailed a cab. She couldn't believe she'd told Trent she loved him. What a total idiot. At least she'd been smart enough to stop him from responding.

Not that his lack of response had stopped her from guessing at what he would have said. Trent Tanford was kind and caring and an incredible lover, but he just didn't seem like the kind of man who said "I love you" or even entertained the thought.

A cab shot to the curb and stopped with a catlike screech of the brakes. Carrie jumped in and quickly rattled off the address to the driver.

She settled back against the seat, watched the driver maneuver in the heavy traffic and continued spinning thoughts in her head. If Trent had been able to respond the other night, he probably would've said something gentlemanly and evasive like, "Thank you. I think you're amazing."

Carrie's shoulders slumped forward.

Or maybe he would've given her a wide, dimpled grin and a long speech about himself and what he wanted and didn't want in his life. How, even though he cared about her, they'd made a deal, a yearly plan, and he couldn't see past that right now....

Carrie felt light-headed. The air in the cab wasn't much better than the air outside.

It really sucked to be in love.

Or maybe it just sucked to be in love by yourself.

When the cab pulled up to her mother's building, she thanked the driver and gave him a nice healthy tip with his fare. Then she jogged up the stairs and arrived at her mother's door with an unattractive sheen of sweat on her brow.

Wanda was in the kitchen with her head in the cupboard that housed the plates and bowls. She pulled back when she heard Carrie come in. "Hello there."

"Hey." Carrie smiled, dropped her purse on the nearby hall table. "How's it going? Everything okay?"

"Everything's copacetic," Wanda announced good-naturedly, using one of her favorite new words because after a while saying "fine" and "good" to describe Rachel's doings and mood during the day got boring.

Wanda was living in now, something Carrie had wanted forever, but couldn't afford or convince her mother that she needed. Hell, Rachel wouldn't even consider Carrie being around her that often, much less a nonfamily member. But as Rachel's condition had grown worse over the past few months, Carrie had started to worry about her mother's safety from 10:00 p.m. to 6:00 a.m. Thankfully, Rachel had finally come to accept the idea of Wanda living in her home full-time, and that made Carrie feel so much better.

"So, I thought we could order some dinner tonight," Carrie said, eyeing the junk drawer where they used to keep all the take-out menus when she was a kid.

"Already been ordered," Wanda informed her, taking plates and glasses out of the cupboards and placing them on the counter. "Should be here any minute now."

"Oh, great. What did you order?"

"I didn't."

"What?" Carrie asked, confused.

Wanda looked sheepish. "Dinner has been ordered every night. It comes promptly at seven."

Carrie shook her head. "I don't understand."

Wanda paused, a knife and fork in her hand. "Mr.

Tanford set it up. He said with all I have to do around here, I shouldn't be cooking three meals a day. I told him I didn't mind, but he insisted."

Carrie couldn't believe what she was hearing. "When did he say that?"

"A few days ago. He was here for a quick visit during his lunch hour."

Again, she was completely stunned. "Trent didn't tell me he was here or about the dinners."

She shrugged. "Maybe he wanted to surprise you."

"He did."

Trent had been here? On his lunch hour?

But why hadn't he mentioned it to her?

For one brief second, she felt that familiar rush to mistrust him enter her system, but she quickly pushed it aside. Who cares why he came and if he forgot to tell her? He had been here. That was enough.

"The food comes with a server and everything," Wanda said brightly. "Oh, your mother's awake, by the way. She had a lovely bath and is resting."

"Thanks, Wanda."

Carrie walked down the hall and entered her mother's bedroom. The first thing she saw was her mother's face. She looked so young—pale, but young. Her gray hair was pulled back off her face and she looked pretty and lucid. But maybe Carrie was just seeing what she wanted to see.

"Hi, Mom."

Rachel's gaze lifted, and Carrie saw recognition. "Carrie?"

Carrie's eyes filled with tears. These moments were so few and far between lately that when they did come Carrie was filled with equal parts of thankfulness and rage.

She went to sit beside the bed. "My very nice husband has ordered the three of us dinner. Would you like to talk while we eat or watch something?"

"Carrie, dear?"

"What, Mom?"

Rachel shook her head. "I have something."

"What it is?"

"A pain."

Carrie's heart dropped. "Where? Show me."

Rachel pointed to her heart.

"How bad?" Carrie asked, fully panicked now.

"It's because your father left."

And then a different kind of panic moved in, sharing space with the sad, angry heart. "I know, Mom. It was a long time ago."

"He left because of me."

"You shouldn't be thinking about this right now." Out in the hall, the doorbell rang. "The food's here. Maybe it's that garlic bread with the chucks of roasted garlic you like so—"

Rachel grabbed Carrie's arm, squeezed until her fingers were white. "I have to think now. I have to talk about it now."

Carrie's throat ached at the sight of her mother's desperation. She didn't want her getting so upset that she had another episode like the other night, but she also understood the rush to explain. Her mother needed to say whatever she needed to say. Now. Because there might not be a later.

Carrie nodded. "Okay."

Rachel sighed, looked thankful. "I asked him to go, Carrie. You didn't know that, did you?"

"No."

"I was so tired of his threats. Every day. But most of all, the way it made you feel every time he said he was going to leave. I couldn't allow that to continue. One night, I said to him, 'Just go. Go now.'" Rachel looked up, her eyes brimming with tears. "And he did."

Carrie put her hand over her mother's and said with impassioned truthfulness, "I'm glad you did."

"But he didn't say goodbye to you," she said sadly, releasing Carrie's wrist. "I will never forgive myself for that."

"You have to forgive yourself. Just like I had to forgive myself for wishing he'd leave."

Her eyes wide, Rachel stared at her.

Carrie pushed on, glad to finally have a chance to release her own hidden guilt. "I couldn't stand it anymore, either. I prayed every night before I went to sleep that he'd leave. That morning, when I woke up to just you, I was…relieved, excited to start a new life. I missed him, don't get me wrong, but as I grew up my memories of him were far better than the reality of him actually being there. Do you understand?"

Rachel nodded, smiled, looked like her old self for a moment. "I do."

Then Wanda and the server came in with a tray full of delicious-smelling food, and Carrie silently thanked Trent for making life a little easier for them all.

They made it a foursome, insisting the server sit down and share their meal with them. Halfway through, Rachel smiled at her daughter and suggested they all watch a movie.

"Your choice, Mom," Carrie said, nibbling on a bread stick.

"To Sir With Love?"

Carrie laughed, but got up to get the DVD from the cabinet. "Listen up, everyone, just so you know what you're in for, this will be two hours of hearing my lovesick mother say how beautiful Sidney Poitier is."

Wanda grinned. "I'm up for that."

The server shrugged. "He is gorgeous."

Rachel smiled at her daughter. "Not to worry, hon, two hours go by quickly with that man on the screen."

Too quickly, Carrie thought as she dropped the disk into the player and switched on the television. In two hours, Sidney would be gone, Wanda would be on her way to bed, Carrie would be going home, and Rachel Gray might be slipping away, back inside her damaged mind once again.

Eleven

He had a wife.

She slept in his bed.

And he was okay with that.

Actually, Trent mused as he stared across the pillow at her, he was more than okay with that. He was over-the-moon about that.

The early-morning sun was crawling up the sky, inch by inch, its pale rays streaming through the windows, backlighting his beautiful bride in a haloesque glow. His sexy little angel, who had come to earth to save him from himself. And hopefully, while she was here with him he could spoil her, give her his protection and his loyalty, and offer her what was left of his heart.

She stirred, inhaled deeply.

Trent felt ready to spring. She was lying on her side, nude, hugging the sheet between her legs, and he wanted to know what her skin felt like, tasted like at 6:00 a.m. He leaned forward and kissed her softly, first her shoulder, then her upper arm.

Her eyes opened. She blinked, trying to register where she was and what was happening to her. When she saw Trent, her gaze cleared and she smiled.

"Morning."

Trent moved in closer, lying on his side, facing her, nearly nose to nose. "Hey." He brushed his nose across hers.

"Good sleep?"

"Very good. You?"

"The best." She reached up and touched his face. "Hey, my knight in Versace armor?"

He chuckled. "What?"

"Thank you."

"For what?"

She wrapped one leg around his waist and pulled him even closer. "I was at my mother's last night, and I had a lovely meal with her and Wanda—and the server."

"Uh-huh."

"Come on. The server who brought the dinner you ordered."

He chuckled. "It's nothing. She should have every comfort." And so should you, he thought, trailing a hand up her soft thigh. "Oh, I forgot to mention something about your mother."

"What?" she asked lazily.

"I went to visit her the other day, during lunch. I didn't tell you because I thought it might make you feel bad."

She came up on one elbow, alert now. "Why?"

He shrugged. "With your new job, I know you don't have the time to go over there as much as you used to, and I didn't want you to feel pressured to try and make it if I went. I'm sure you're working through lunches. Right?"

She nodded.

"I'd like to continue to visit her if you don't mind."

"Mind? Are you crazy or just—" she leaned down and kissed him "—totally amazing?" She pushed him onto his back and climbed on top of him. "Or are you both?"

"What I am," he said with a growl of need, "is very happy you're sitting on top of me."

She grinned, clearly feeling the hard and ready length of him against her bottom. "I'm going out on a huge limb here."

"Damn fine way of stroking my ego, sweetheart."

She rolled her eyes. "Big fan of double entendres, are you?"

"That one, I am." He laughed. "I mean, come on, I'm a guy." He noticed that she wasn't laughing and he asked, "You okay, sweetheart?"

"I want you, Trent."

"Good," he assured her.

"No, I mean I want you. Not for just a year." She released a breath, looked at the ceiling for a second. "God, I'm horrible at this."

Heat ripped into his gut and his heart. "You're doing just fine."

Her eyes glittered like emeralds as she stared down at him, vulnerable as an infant. "I want this, you and our marriage."

Trent stilled. He wasn't at all sure of what to say or how he felt.

"I've shocked you," she said.

"A little," he admitted.

"And you want to get out of this bed and calmly tell me that we had an agreement. And while you like me, and are attracted to me, you in no way want to—"

"Stop, Carrie. You're spinning."

She couldn't meet his eyes. "I should get in the shower."

She tried to get off him, but Trent wasn't going to let her get away. "Talk to me. Stay here and talk to me."

He held her hips, and after a moment, she met his gaze. "All right."

"As you were saying."

She released a weighty breath. "I think we're great together. I don't want to be with anyone else; I can't imagine it—ever." She swallowed nervously. "What do you think?"

"I think," he said as he reached up, curled a wedge of her hair around his fingers, "okay."

"Okay?" she repeated.

He looked into her eyes and nodded. He was, if nothing else, a man of his word.

Then he coaxed her to him and kissed her as if she was his, for more than a year, for a lifetime.

At three that afternoon, a bouquet of flowers was delivered to Carrie's cubicle, pink peonies so artfully arranged they looked like a still-life painting sitting there on her desk. She knew instantly they were from Trent, and she smiled as she opened the card.

Meet me tonight.
7 p.m.
727 5th Ave
I'll be the one holding the blue box.

Curious and unable to wait until seven, Carrie swiveled in her chair and looked up the address on Google. What was life like before the Internet, she wondered as she impatiently waited for the location to appear on the screen.

Then she saw it, where she was supposed to meet Trent tonight, and a shot of excitement went off inside of her, like fireworks against a diamond sky. It was an excitement that only a girl could truly understand.

She glanced at the time and frowned.

Four tediously long hours to go...

He saw her before she saw him, walking quickly down the street, wearing a stylish white pantsuit and black heels.

The store had just closed, and his surprise was going to be arriving at any moment. He was amazed that he could pull this off. But everything, even the famous Tiffany's store, was for rent for the right price. True, the whole thing was a bit corny and had been in done in a movie or two, but the place was also classic New York.

He watched the security guard lead Carrie through the closed steel doors. And then she was in front of him with a slightly worried smile on her lips. "Are we breaking and entering?"

He chuckled. "No. Security is outside, as you saw, and there are more of them watching upstairs. And somewhere around here there's a salesperson, but they're being discreet."

She looked around, her gaze resting on case after case of expensive jewelry. "What are we doing here?"

"Ever heard of *Breakfast at Tiffany's?*"

"Of course."

He took her hand. "Well, this is going to be Dinner at Tiffany's."

Her eyes bulged. "Are you serious?"

"As a heart attack."

Trent led her into the main room, where a dining table was set up, complete with white linens, silver flatware and more pink peonies.

Carrie stared at him. "I cannot believe that we're having dinner here. In the store. Surrounded by every precious stone and metal there is."

He nodded. "Then we have some shopping to do."

"What?" she said, shaking her head and laughing at the insanity of it all.

"I thought it was about time."

"Time for what?"

"Look at your finger."

Grinning mischievously, Carrie held up her hands and wiggled them. "Which one?"

He pointed to the ring finger on her left hand. "There's no ring on it, honey."

"Yours, either," she pointed out.

"I always thought that if I ever did get married, I'd never wear a ring."

She lifted her brows. "Interesting. And what do you think now?"

He gathered her in his arms and kissed her. "I'm thinking I want you to pick one out for me."

She smiled. "Okay."

"And I'll pick out one for you."

She smiled wider. "Okay."

Behind them, the two-person catering staff hovered, waiting to serve them. So Trent left Carrie's side, walked around the table and held out her chair for her.

She sat with a gracious thank-you to her host and put her napkin in her lap with a great flourish. Trent smiled at her. It pleased him to no end that she was enjoying herself so much.

When the waitstaff had set the meal before them, Carrie looked up, her expression a mixture of surprise and eagerness.

"Pizza?" she exclaimed.

"I thought you loved pizza."

"I do. It's perfect! This whole night is perfect."

"Pizza and Tiffany's. Classic New York."

As they ate, they talked. About work, travel, family. Up until this point, Trent had shared little about his mother and father, mostly because he didn't know all that much about them as people. But he did tell Carrie about his beloved nanny growing up and their crazy escapades in the city, and the one time they took the ferry to Staten Island and got so lost they missed the return ferry and had to spend the night at her cousin's house.

Best time of his life, he told Carrie. "Except for maybe right now."

She smiled and took another bite of her slice.

When Trent's cell phone rang, they were deep in conversation about her mother's artwork, and he let it go. But soon the beeping of a waiting text had him glancing down. "Sorry about this."

"Everything okay?" Carrie asked.

He stared at the screen. "Nothing vital. Just one of my assistants is leaving for the day."

"One of your assistants? I didn't know you had more than one."

"I have four."

"Wow. Nice promotion."

"I know it sounds crazy, but they're all vital. My workload has tripled since the promotion. Not that I'm complaining. Anyway, she stayed late to finish some paperwork I needed to have completed first thing in the morning."

"Ah. Well, it was good of her to check in. Very professional."

He heard the thin strain of unease in his wife's voice, and he dropped the phone back in his pocket and looked at her. "I wanted no interruptions tonight, but unfortunately the head of AMS doesn't get to be off duty."

"I understand," she said, her gaze flickering from him to her plate.

"It can be frustrating at times. You sure you still want to hang out with me?"

She pretended to think about it. Then she laughed and said, "Absolutely."

He reached across the table and took her hand. "I'm here with you."

It took her a second to respond, but finally, she nodded. "I know." Then she gestured around herself. "I just can't believe you did this."

"Anything for you."

She laced her fingers with his and smiled broadly.

"Are you happy, Carrie?" he asked.

"I'm with you, Tanford. That always makes me happy. Now, will you pass the red pepper flakes?"

"Oh my good Lord."

"Are you going to stare at that thing all night?"

"Don't call her a thing."

They were in bed. Trent was reading, and Carrie was staring at her ring as though it was a newborn and she wanted to memorize its face. Trent looked down his sexy black reading glasses at her. "It's a her?"

"Yes, and now you've hurt her feelings."

He snorted, took her hand in his. "You're a nut, but I love to see you so happy."

"I am and I don't ever want to be not happy again."

He examined the ring, the pretty diamond trellis band he'd picked out for her after seeing her nearly burst into tears when she spotted it behind the glass. "It's very unassuming—sorry, she's very unassuming."

"I'm not a big-rock kinda girl. This ring is me, us, perfection." She turned into him, her leg sliding across his pajama-clad thighs. It was her standard move, and she knew he loved it. "You have great taste, by the way."

He put his arm around her. "I had nothing to do with it, but thanks."

"Do you like yours?"

"I do. But I like what you had engraved on it more."

"Ah, yes." She cleared her throat and made it dramatic. *"A day, a year, forever.* Damn, I'm good." When he laughed, she looked up at him. "You haven't changed your mind about that, have you? The forever part?"

"You mean after watching you talk to your ring and call it 'she'? Surprisingly, no."

"Good man." Grinning, she reached up and slipped off his glasses. "Make love to me."

"Shh…" He was over her in seconds. "Not in front of the ring."

Carrie giggled. "She's cool. She likes to watch."

"Hmm." His mouth met hers. "Kinky."

Twelve

Trent left the police station for the third time that month, BlackBerry in hand. He nodded a silent good-bye to his attorney and stepped into his town car. It had been the same series of questions to start, with one ridiculous new one to end. McGray had asked Trent if the letter he'd received had come to his home or office, and what kind of paper both the letter and envelope were made of.

Trent had offered the man everything he could recall, but McGray seemed frustrated when he'd finally told Trent he could leave.

They were obviously no closer to solving the mystery of Marie's death.

The driver maneuvered through the heavy evening traffic. Trent had already had a full day of work, then his meeting with police, and now he was off to Pacheco restaurant. He was meeting with two long-standing advertisers and the top members of their staffs for a dinner party at the Spanish restaurant. He had wanted Carrie to come with him, but she had already offered Wanda a night off, so she was staying with her mom until pretty late.

He hated going solo to social events now.

He grinned, shook his head. What a switch.

And he really wanted her there tonight more than ever, because his father was going to be in attendance, symbolically passing the torch in front of his oldest advertisers.

But he'd see her later, in bed, and make sure she had a lovely breakfast in the morning.

God, he was such a puss.

It was five minutes to eight when they pulled up in front of the restaurant. Trent got out and headed inside.

It was lunchtime at the Park Café, and two women sat at a small table, drinking lattes and splitting an overly fattening low-fat muffin.

"Check this guy out."

A petite woman with a tight blond bun grabbed the newspaper from her dark-haired friend and thoroughly scanned the pages. "Wow. He's so hot."

"Look at that girl he's with," Dark Hair said in a severely depressed tone. "She's perfect. She's got to be an actress or a model." She sighed. "I could never get a guy like that."

"No normal-looking woman could get a guy like that," Tight Bun said.

"That's because he wouldn't even notice one of us if we walked past him."

After gulping down her coffee, Tight Bun said, "I can't look at either one of them anymore. I have to get to work. Do you want to go to a movie tonight?"

"As opposed to what?" Dark Hair said, grinning. "Bungalow 8?"

Tight Bun snorted. "Yeah, right."

They both laughed, then stood up and left the Park Café, leaving behind their empty coffee cups and the newspaper they'd been ogling.

Carrie sipped her extra hot double cappuccino and watched them go. She'd heard that conversation a thousand times in her own head whenever she'd seen an especially cute guy, an out-of-her-league guy. Hell, she'd thought all of those things when she'd met Trent.

Thank goodness that part of her life was over, she mused, remembering the very satisfying morning she'd spent with her husband, followed by his sweet gesture of serving her breakfast in bed.

Curious, Carrie reached over to their table and swiped the paper. She turned to the entertainment section and looked for the man and the model. When she found them, focused her eyes on the photograph in the center of the page, she felt the breath leave her body. There was a picture of her husband and a beautiful blonde. The pair stood close together, Trent's arm draped around her. He seemed to be about to kiss her cheek.

The headline screamed at her:

The Pretty People Party at Pacheco

Carrie felt cold, numb as she scanned the article for her husband's name and some explanation for why he was with this woman when he was supposed to be having a dinner meeting with a bunch of old men.

Because there had to be a reason, right? He wouldn't lie to her. He wouldn't be running around with some woman when Carrie was hanging out at her sick mother's house.

She pushed back her jealousy and her quick feelings of mistrust. She wasn't going to do that anymore; she'd promised herself. There was an explanation. She just had to find it.

What she found was the article. It read:

Last night at Pacheco, AMS honcho hottie, Trent Tanford got cozy with a beautiful mystery blonde.

With her heart beating anxiously in her belly, Carrie stared at the woman. There was something about her. She looked so familiar.

Carrie squinted. She knew her.

But how? From where?

Was she a model or an actress, like those two women had suggested? Or was it…?

Then she stilled. Like a silent movie playing in her mind, she saw herself, late one night, opening the door to another one of "Trent's Troops." Carrie's shoulders dropped—her heart, too. Mystery Blonde was no longer a mystery. She was one of the women who'd come knocking on her door back in the day looking for Trent.

She tossed the paper back on the girls' table, left her coffee and croissant and walked out of the Park Café.

Why had she allowed herself to fall in love with a playboy? Why couldn't she just have left things alone? Why couldn't she have stuck to her end of the deal, the business arrangement—no sex, no love?

Dammit.

Last night when Carrie had gotten home late from her mother's house, Trent had said that his meeting had gone "well." Obviously. He had changed the subject pretty quickly after that, she recalled.

Amanda's words slithered through her mind. "Don't expect a man to change."

Back in her building, Carrie stabbed the button for the twelfth floor and tried not to think about what she and Trent had done in this elevator not one week ago.

She stalked down the hall and into her apartment. No, it was Trent's apartment. She would have to move in with her mom for now. There was no way she was staying here, with him. Not after this.

She may have been a bought wife, but she would not accept a cheating husband. One that had lied to her and promised his faithfulness.

She packed quickly, then sat down at his desk, took out a piece of paper and pen. For a moment, she wondered if she was acting rationally, if her actions and re-actions were wrong, if this was about her father again.

But even her father with all his faults hadn't cheated on his wife. The facts were there. That blonde had come to Carrie's door in the middle of the night looking for Trent. And Trent had never denied that those women were his lovers.

White-hot anger ripped through her. She was through confronting him, talking things out.

She was done.

After finishing the letter and depositing it on his desk, she grabbed her things and was out the door.

He was a happily married man with a chance at a real family.

The one thing his father had done right by him.

A month ago, it had all been about gaining power and status for Trent. Now it was all about Carrie and building their future and, God help him, maybe a little Trent or Carrie Jr. if his lovely wife was up for that.

Trent walked down the hall at seven-thirty, with a take-out bag in his hand. He had no idea if Carrie liked Thai food, but he thought they could give it a try. Then maybe a movie. The last few nights had been filled with work obligations. Tonight, it would be just the two of them.

But first he had to ply her with a little wine, because he was pretty sure she had seen the daily paper. She hadn't returned any of his calls at work, which meant she was either insanely busy or freezing him out.

Not that he blamed her. He was a huge ass for not warning her. What the hell was he thinking letting his wife be blindsided by that? He'd seen that photographer, but had been too preoccupied by the advertisers and the fact that he'd forgotten some projection sheets at the office.

"Honey, I'm home."

He walked through the dark apartment, checked the bathrooms. Nothing, she wasn't around.

He frowned. Maybe she wasn't home yet. Or perhaps she had stopped by her mother's. He went to his desk and grabbed the phone. But when he saw the note with his name on it, he stopped.

As he read, shock took hold of him and held steady until he'd finished the last word. Then, as he slowly realized what Carrie had done, anger snaked into his blood and dripped from his veins. Yes, she had seen the picture, but instead of talking to him about it, she'd run. She'd run away like her damned father.

Her words the other day had meant nothing. She had no faith in him or the marriage she'd said she wanted so much. But worst of all, she hadn't had the balls to face him and tell him in person.

That he couldn't abide.

His face was a mask of rage as he crushed the note in his fist and tossed it into the trash.

Thirteen

Carrie had been living with her mother for four days when she got a letter from Trent. It was the first she'd heard from him since she'd walked out of their apartment, and out of his life.

There were some papers for her to look over, he'd written, and he was going to leave them at his office for her to pick up.

He'd also included the times of day he would be out of the office, so they wouldn't have to see each other.

Carrie's heart squeezed painfully. These had been the longest four days of her life. She missed him so badly, she ached with it. But clearly he hadn't felt the same.

She stood at the kitchen counter in her suit and stared at his note, typed up, not even handwritten.

Papers for her to look at… What were they? Separation papers? Divorce papers?

He sure wanted this over and done with in a hurry. Maybe he needed to make things less complicated for him and the blonde, she thought bitterly. Maybe the woman had already moved into his apartment, into his bed.

Suddenly, she felt as though a piano was sitting on her chest, intensifying the ache into sweeps of despair and anxiety, and grief for the loss of a wonderful friendship. But she was a stubborn person who wouldn't go crawling back to a man who didn't love her, a man who thought that a little blond candy on the side was okay.

She grabbed her purse and headed out the door to work. She'd stop by his office this afternoon, during one of his "out of the office" times. Might as well get it over with…

"Anything for lunch today?"

Trent glanced up, shook his head. "No, thanks."

Danny, the sandwich guy, didn't move. He just stood in the doorway and waited.

Trent exhaled heavily. He was in no mood for this today. "Nothing personal, Dan. I'm having lunch out."

"With your wife?"

"No," Trent muttered through a tightly clenched jaw. "Not that it's any business of yours."

"That's true."

Trent looked up, glared at the freckle-faced kid who

delivered sandwiches during the day and inhaled law books at night. "What do you want?"

"I want to ask you something."

"Ask then. I have a ton of work here."

Danny rarely walked inside Trent's office, but today he did just that, and sat down across from Trent at his desk. "If I had seemed to change into a machine overnight, a machine who never left the office, would you say something to me?"

Trent stared at him. "Yes. I would say, good for you. You understand how to make it in this city."

Danny snorted. "Maybe you would have said that before…"

"I don't have time for this," Trent snapped.

"You were happy, Trent. Happier than I've ever seen you. What the hell happened?"

Trent glared at him, really pissed off now. "It's Mr. Tanford."

Danny sighed and stood up. "All right, Mr. Tanford. I'm going. But before I do, I just want to say something." Even though Trent shook his head with annoyance, Danny continued, "When you offered to pay for my school a few years ago, my family didn't like it."

Trent scoffed. "Why the hell not?"

"They felt that only family should help family."

"Of course."

"But I told them you were like family to me, like a brother. I told them that family doesn't always come from blood."

"What's your point, brother?" Trent said with far less hostility than a moment ago.

"My point is that you may not have had the kind of family you wanted as a kid, but you can have it now."

Trent nodded. "That's a nice thought, Danny."

"She's your family."

"Stop." Trent shook his head. "Go now. I have to get back to work. I'll see you tomorrow."

When Danny left, Trent attempted to regain his train of thought, but it was impossible. Danny's words had thrown him off, made him for one second believe that he could actually have what the boy had suggested. A family. With her.

Then reality faced him head-on. He hadn't had one as a child, as a young adult, and he wouldn't have one now. Those kinds of dreams were for starry-eyed kids and Disneyland-loving adults.

The woman he'd given his heart to had thrown it back in his face.

As Trent stared at his computer screen, a thought, a question, snaked into his mind without invitation. It was a question he didn't even want to look at, because it might make him partly responsible for her leaving.

Yes, Carrie had gripped tightly to those fears of hers, but how much had Trent really tried to help alleviate them? He, too, had hidden things from her, like the meeting with the police. He hadn't laid his life bare and open for her. Was it possible that he had a few fears of his own?

He shook his head, trying to clear his thoughts, but

it was an impossible task. The idea that he might have wronged Carrie in some way, or their relationship, was now permanently embedded in his mind, right alongside an image of her face, that sweet, laughing face he knew he would never be able to forget.

The woman behind the desk asked if Carrie could wait just a moment. Carrie nodded at Trent's secretary and took a seat in the waiting area. She felt sick to her stomach. What was she doing here? she wondered miserably. Getting some papers? Something that legally called off their "deal"?

The door to the hallway was open, and Carrie could hear Trent's secretary talking to someone. Carrie turned and glanced over her shoulder. All she could see were balloons and high heels. But then, whoever was holding the bouquet of balloons handed them off to Trent's secretary, and Carrie was able to see the previous owner perfectly.

Oh my God!

The blonde from the photograph.

Carrie jumped up. Unbridled anger swirled through her, and she could hardly breathe. On unsteady legs, she walked to the door.

The blonde continued to talk to Trent's secretary. She didn't see Carrie coming. And then Carrie was in her face, seething with rage and a ruined heart.

"You," Carrie blurted out, facing the exceptionally beautiful young woman.

"Mrs. Tanford?" Trent's secretary looked worried. "If you'll just have a seat, I'll be right with you."

"Mrs. Tanford?" the blonde asked with a genuine smile. She put her hand out to Carrie. "Hi, I'm one of Mr. Tanford's assistants. I don't think we've met."

Carrie sniffed. "Oh, we've met." His assistant. Nice cover.

The woman's brows snapped together. "I'm sorry?"

"Are you? Are you sorry you ruined a marriage?"

Trent's secretary gasped, and the blonde looked shocked. "I think you have me confused with someone else."

"No, I think I remember you grabbing my husband in the newspaper."

The blonde shook her head. "No, no, no. The picture was completely misleading."

"Of course it was."

"The restaurant was very loud. Mr. Tanford was leaning in, telling me to go back to the office and get a file he'd forgotten."

Carrie snorted, shrugged. "Sure, that would seem totally logical if I didn't also remember you coming to my door in the middle of the night looking for Trent."

"That was several weeks ago, right?"

"That's right."

"I was looking for Mr. Tanford."

Carrie exhaled. This woman was as dim as a box of rocks. "I know. I just said that."

She shook her head. "No, I used to be the senior Mr.

Tanford's assistant. He couldn't find his son that night, and he sent me out looking for him. But I apologize for disturbing you. Really."

Something started to work in Carrie's chest, a heat swirling around and around like water in a toilet, warning her that perhaps she had made a huge mistake. "But the senior Mr. Tanford is retired."

Another woman came up to them, a gift in her hand. "Lauren, we have to go. Everyone's waiting."

The blonde, who Carrie now knew was Lauren, turned back to her and said, "My shower."

"Shower?" Carrie uttered weakly. "As in baby or wedding?"

"Both actually." Lauren touched Carrie's arm and explained her situation. "When Mr. Tanford retired, I was going to be out of a job. Soon-to-be married, pregnant and out of a job. Not good."

Carrie's knees threatened to buckle.

Lauren continued, "The new Mr. Tanford said he'd keep me on, and after the baby comes, too. My fiancé is still in medical school, so we don't have the greatest income right now. This company has great benefits."

If she could've given herself a superpower in that moment, she would have made herself invisible. But she was no Superwoman; she was in fact deeply flawed. She shook her head, closed her eyes for a second. "I'm such a jerk. A stupid, jealous, insecure jerk."

Trent's secretary snorted. "We've all been there, honey."

"I'm so sorry," Carrie said to Lauren.

The woman smiled. "It's okay."

"It's not, but thanks. And you can expect an enormous baby gift from me. A stroller or crib or a new house or something."

Lauren laughed. "You're funny. It's no wonder that Mr. Tanford's always trying to get home early."

Carrie felt as though she'd been stabbed. She needed to leave and quickly. She turned to Trent's secretary. "I'll be out of your hair as soon as possible. Trent left me some papers…"

The woman nodded. "They're on Mr. Tanford's desk. Do you want me to get them or—"

"I'll go myself. Thanks."

After another quick apology to Lauren, Carrie turned around and headed back into the waiting room and then into Trent's office.

She stood there for a moment, trying to get hold of herself after that debacle with Lauren.

Then she glanced around. Of course, Trent wasn't there. Yet, he was everywhere. His taste, his colors, his scent. She wanted him. So badly, she wanted him. But she knew after what she'd done and how she'd acted, she didn't deserve him.

She fingered the envelope on his desk. Her name was on it, in his handwriting. She dreaded what was inside of it. But she knew even before she opened it. Divorce papers.

She wanted to throw up. Again.

Everything was here, the year's agreement.

Oh, Trent...

He wasn't going back on anything he'd offered her. She sighed. She didn't care about that. She wouldn't accept anything more from him.

But it was what he'd included on the next page that brought tears to her eyes. Trent was going to pay for her mother's medical expenses and her care for the rest of her life.

Carrie put the envelope back down on his desk, walked out of the office and left the papers unsigned.

Fourteen

"What the hell is she playing at, Devlin? Does she want more money?" Trent sat in his lawyer's office, and stared across the desk at the man, who looked utterly nonplussed.

"She says she wants nothing from you."

"Not possible," Trent muttered darkly.

"She says she won't sign the papers unless you remove every bit of support that you've offered."

Trent cursed. "I'm not going to do that."

Devlin shrugged. "Why are you fighting this? It's every man's dream."

"This is hardly a dream, Jerry. To me, this is a damned nightmare. A week ago, I was happy. My wife was happy. She loved me. I…"

"What?" Jerry asked, hopelessly confused by his wishy-washy client.

Trent shook his head, stared out the window.

"What do you want to do, Mr. Tanford?" Devlin pressed, his hand poised over the unsigned divorce papers.

"I want to end this," Trent ground out. "This whole damn thing."

"That's what I'm trying to help you do. End your marriage."

"No, Jerry. I want to end *this,* this conversation. My marriage?" He stood up and grabbed his briefcase. "That I want back."

Hanging out on a Wednesday evening on Staten Island was a first for Carrie, but she figured she was about to embark on a good many firsts tonight and she was just planning on going for it.

She stood outside of Denino's Pizzeria Tavern waiting for Trent, nervous to her core, but knowing that what she had to say to him, what she had to propose, was good and right.

"This is an interesting place to meet."

Oh, that voice, she had missed it so much. She looked up to find him walking toward her, his gait long and purposeful. He was dressed casually in jeans and a white shirt, looking as he always looked: tall, handsome and formidable.

She tried for a light mood. "I thought you loved pizza."

His blue eyes darkened, indicating he was not in the mood for light anything. "What's up, Carrie? You didn't take the deal."

"I said I'd sign the papers."

"I don't care about the papers. What I want to know is why you wouldn't let me help you."

Her heart squeezed, and she just wanted to run to him, bury her face in his chest. "Why do you want to help me, Trent? Why not just get out without any strings?"

He shook his head. "I can't do that."

"Why not?" she said gently.

"I'm not that kind of guy."

Carrie cocked her head to one side. "Are you sure that's the reason?"

"What do you mean?" he said defensively, leaning against the exterior wall of the restaurant.

Behind them, a group of customers left the restaurant, walking off toward their cars with the scent of tomato sauce and garlic following after them.

Carrie gazed up at Trent. "Maybe you want to take care of me and my mom, keep those strings attached because you love me."

"Carrie—"

"You love me like I love you, and you really don't want this to end, but your pride is hurt, and I get that. You should be hurt. I hurt you, I panicked, and I'm so sorry—"

He pounded the wall with his fist. "You walked out on me."

"I know," she said softly. "And it was wrong and stupid, but I don't think it should end our marriage."

He looked around, gestured. "Why are we here? Staten Island."

"That story you told me about your nanny. How she brought you here on the greatest day of your life. I thought we should be here because it's the only story I know."

Anger slipped from Trent's features. "What?"

"We fell for each other right away, hot and heavy. We had a friendship, too, that's true, but we didn't go deep, Trent."

He raised a brow, and she laughed. "Yes, we had great sex, but we didn't swap stories. The way we got married was unconventional, to say the least. We didn't get our time."

"Our time for what?"

"To get to know each other. I don't know your history, your childhood, what makes you the man I love, what makes you…you." She took a step toward him, looking hopeful. "I realized that the reason I was so insecure about loving you was because I didn't have the security of knowing you—your history, your life."

"It's not a great history," he said softly.

She reached out, touched his cheek. "I don't care. It's yours and I love you."

His jaw tightened, and then he nodded. "I love you, too."

Tears pricked her eyes. She'd wanted to hear those three words from him for so long, and hearing them right now was the best present, the best reason to hope she could ever imagine.

"Good," she said, her heart racing. "Because I want to offer you a new deal."

His brow lifted. "A new deal?"

She nodded, took a deep breath, her gaze holding steady with his. "I want to offer you my love, my heart, my honesty, my commitment to this marriage, and all of my stories."

Trent reached for her then and gently pulled her into his arms. "And what do I have to give you?"

"The same," she uttered, letting her head fall against his chest.

He sighed. "I'm sorry I didn't tell you about the police and about the photographer. My whole life my parents, especially my father, seemed to jump to the conclusion that I was to blame, always to blame. I couldn't risk that with you."

"It's okay," she assured him.

"I held back. I get that." He brushed a kiss on the top of her head. "I was falling in love with you and I refused to acknowledge it."

She shook her head. "It's done. Over. Today, right here, let's start over." She lifted her head, stared up into his denim-blue eyes. "Take the deal, Tanford, and not only do we both get the history, but we get to create the future, too."

He gathered her in his arms and held her against him. "Oh my God, I love you. I was going insane without you, Carrie."

"Me, too."

"I never took my ring off. I'm such a hack."

"Then I'm a hack, too," she laughed, "because I never took my ring off, either."

He tipped her face up and kissed her, a soft, tender kiss that spoke of love and held the promise of an honest, open future. "Marry me again?"

Tears sprang to Carrie's eyes and she nodded. "Yes."

"A church wedding?"

"Yes."

He kissed her again, and this time it was raw and passion filled.

Behind them, a couple walked out of the restaurant and the woman snorted and said drily, "Get a room," before walking down the street.

Carrie and Trent broke out in laughter.

"Are you hungry?" he asked her. "Do you want some pizza?"

"I am hungry," she said, wrapping her arms around his waist once more, breathing in the scent of him. "For pizza, for you, for our life together, and for those slightly disturbing stories of you as a bad little boy."

He grinned. Oh, those dimples. "Why don't we start with the pizza, then work our way down that list, okay?"

"Absolutely," she said, curling into him as they walked into Denino's, ready to begin again, starting with a little pizza pie, and a night that was truly classic New York.

* * * * *

The Colton family is back!
Enjoy a sneak preview of
COLTON'S SECRET SERVICE
by Marie Ferrarella,
part of
THE COLTONS: FAMILY FIRST *miniseries.*

Available from Silhouette Romantic Suspense
in September 2008.

He cautioned himself to be leery. He was human and he'd been conned before. But never by anyone nearly so attractive. Never by anyone he'd felt so attracted to.

In her defense, Nick supposed that Georgie could actually be telling him the truth. That she was a victim in all this. He had his people back in California checking her out, to make sure she was who she said she was and had, as she claimed, not even been near a computer but on the road these last few months that the threats had been made.

In the meantime, he was doing his own checking out. Up close and exceedingly personal. So personal he could feel his blood stirring.

It had been a long time since he'd thought of himself

as anything other than a law enforcement agent of one type or other. But Georgeann Grady made him remember that beneath the oaths he had taken and his devotion to duty, there beat the heart of a man.

A man who'd been far too long without the touch of a woman.

He watched as the light from the fireplace caressed the outline of Georgie's small, trim, jean-clad body as she moved about the rustic living room that could have easily come off the set of a Hollywood Western. Except that it was genuine.

As genuine as she claimed to be?

Something inside of him hoped so.

He wasn't supposed to be taking sides. His only interest in being here was to guarantee Senator Joe Colton's safety as the latter continued to make his bid for the presidency. Everything else was supposed to be secondary, but, Nick had to silently admit, that was just a wee bit hard to remember right now.

Earlier, before she'd put her precocious handful of a daughter to bed, Georgie had fed his appetite by whipping up some kind of a delicious concoction out of the vegetables she'd pulled from her garden. Vegetables that, by all rights, should have been withered and dried. She'd mentioned that a friend came by on occasion to weed and tend it. Still, it surprised him that somehow she'd managed to make something mouthwatering out of it.

Almost as mouthwatering as she looked to him right at this moment.

Again, he was reminded of the appetite that hadn't been fed, hadn't been satisfied.

And wasn't going to be, Nick sternly told himself. At least not now. Maybe later, when things took on a more definite shape and all the questions in his head were answered to his satisfaction, there would be time to explore this feeling. This woman. But not now.

Damn it.

"Sorry about the lack of light," Georgie said, breaking into his train of thought as she turned around to face him. If she noticed the way he was looking at her, she gave no indication. "But I don't see a point in paying for electricity if I'm not going to be here. Besides, Emmie really enjoys camping out. She likes roughing it."

"And you?" Nick asked, moving closer to her, so close that a whisper would have trouble fitting in. "What do you like?"

The very breath stopped in Georgie's throat as she looked up at him.

"I think you've got a fair shot of guessing that one," she told him softly.

* * * * *

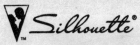

Silhouette®

Romantic
SUSPENSE

**Sparked by Danger,
Fueled by Passion.**

The Coltons Are Back!

Marie Ferrarella
Colton's Secret Service

The Coltons: Family First

On a mission to protect a senator, Secret Service agent
Nick Sheffield tracks down a threatening message only
to discover Georgie Gradie Colton, a rodeo-riding single
mom, who insists on her innocence. Nick is instantly
taken with the feisty redhead, but vows not to let his
feelings interfere with his mission. Now he must figure
out if this woman is conning him or if he can trust her
and the passion they share....

Available September wherever books are sold.

**Look for upcoming Colton titles
from Silhouette Romantic Suspense:**

RANCHER'S REDEMPTION by Beth Cornelison, Available October
THE SHERIFF'S AMNESIAC BRIDE by Linda Conrad, Available November
SOLDIER'S SECRET CHILD by Caridad Piñeiro, Available December
BABY'S WATCH by Justine Davis, Available January 2009
A HERO OF HER OWN by Carla Cassidy, Available February 2009

Visit Silhouette Books at www.eHarlequin.com SRS27598

REQUEST YOUR FREE BOOKS!

2 FREE NOVELS PLUS 2 FREE GIFTS!

Silhouette® *Desire*®

Passionate, Powerful, Provocative!

YES! Please send me 2 FREE Silhouette Desire® novels and my 2 FREE gifts (gifts are worth about $10). After receiving them, if I don't wish to receive any more books, I can return the shipping statement marked "cancel". If I don't cancel, I will receive 6 brand-new novels every month and be billed just $4.05 per book in the U.S. or $4.74 per book in Canada, plus 25¢ shipping and handling per book and applicable taxes, if any*. That's a savings of almost 15% off the cover price! I understand that accepting the 2 free books and gifts places me under no obligation to buy anything. I can always return a shipment and cancel at any time. Even if I never buy another book, the two free books and gifts are mine to keep forever.

225 SDN ERVX 326 SDN ERVM

Name	(PLEASE PRINT)	
Address		Apt. #
City	State/Prov.	Zip/Postal Code

Signature (if under 18, a parent or guardian must sign)

Mail to the Silhouette Reader Service:
IN U.S.A.: P.O. Box 1867, Buffalo, NY 14240-1867
IN CANADA: P.O. Box 609, Fort Erie, Ontario L2A 5X3

Not valid to current subscribers of Silhouette Desire books.

Want to try two free books from another line?
Call 1-800-873-8635 or visit www.morefreebooks.com.

* Terms and prices subject to change without notice. N.Y. residents add applicable sales tax. Canadian residents will be charged applicable provincial taxes and GST. Offer not valid in Quebec. This offer is limited to one order per household. All orders subject to approval. Credit or debit balances in a customer's account(s) may be offset by any other outstanding balance owed by or to the customer. Please allow 4 to 6 weeks for delivery. Offer available while quantities last.

Your Privacy: Silhouette Books is committed to protecting your privacy. Our Privacy Policy is available online at www.eHarlequin.com or upon request from the Reader Service. From time to time we make our lists of customers available to reputable third parties who may have a product or service of interest to you. If you would prefer we not share your name and address, please check here. ☐

SDES08R

COMING NEXT MONTH

#1891 PRINCE OF MIDTOWN—Jennifer Lewis
Park Avenue Scandals
This royal had only one way to keep his dedicated—and lovely—
assistant under his roof...seduce her into his bed!

#1892 THE M.D.'S MISTRESS—Joan Hohl
Gifts from a Billionaire
Finally she was with the sexy surgeon she'd always loved. But
would their affair last longer than the week?

#1893 BABY BONANZA—Maureen Child
Billionaires and Babies
Secret twin babies? A carefree billionaire discovers he's a
daddy—but is he ready to become a groom?

#1894 WED BY DECEPTION—Emilie Rose
The Payback Affairs
The husband she'd believed dead was back—and very much alive.
And determined to make her his...at any cost.

#1895 HIS EXPECTANT EX—Catherine Mann
The Landis Brothers
The ink was not yet dry on their divorce papers when she
discovered she was pregnant. Could a baby bring them a second
chance?

#1896 THE DESERT KING—Olivia Gates
Throne of Judar
Forced to marry to save his throne, this desert king could not deny
the passion he felt for his bride of *in*convenience.

SDCNM0808